Dear Angelina

REINVENTING JENNA ROSE

By *Joni Marie Iraci*

All best wishes always

With gratitude

xx Joni Marie Iraci

REINVENTING JENNA ROSE:
Fat Dog Books

Published by
Fat Dog Books
California, USA

Fat Dog Books
ISBN: 978-0-9991370-4-8

Fiction/Literary
Printed in the United States of America

Visit our website at www.fatdogbooks.com

DEDICATION

To Joe — the root of all the things wild and wonderful in my life and to my children, Nic Iraci, Liza and Drew Engberg for their tireless devotion and for my new grandson, Grayson for lighting up my life.

ACKNOWLEDGEMENT

After five years of labor, I'm proud to deliver this completed novel. The following wonderful people were instrumental in keeping it and me on track: Sarah Lawrence College Professor Ilya Wachs for reading all my stories and advising me to "get on it." Novelist Carol Zoref for telling me I could write. Novelist Martha Southgate, my mentor at the inception of this novel for her support and guidance. Sarah Lawrence College Professors Neil Arditi, David Castriota, Carolyn Ferrell, Kevin Landdeck and Bill Shullenberger for giving me the platform to fine tune my writing skills and for their gentle nudges. Writer Joann Smith for her endless support.

Novelist and Columbia University Professor Binnie Kirshenbaum for being ever-ready to advise, guide, support, encourage, console, and share her broad knowledge and expertise. Award-winning short story writer and Columbia Professor Deborah Eisenberg for supporting this endeavor in workshop and beyond and for gently critiquing this old lady student. Novelist and Columbia Professor Ben Metcalf for his encouraging critiques and for intuiting that I would follow his advice to, "roll up my sleeves and rewrite" yet again. Columbia Professor and 2018 National Book Award Winner, Novelist Sigrid Nunez for all the encouragement and the inspiring seminars. Director Bill Wadsworth, Playwright Clarence Coo and Administrator John McShane for all that they do for all the Columbia writers all the time and for doing it amazingly well. Laila Maher for supporting all the ancillary things that kept me afloat at Columbia. My Columbia University thesis workshop Professor, Novelist Rebecca Godfrey and the fellow writers who helped this novel take shape with their brilliant suggestions and feedback: Afia Atakora, Courtney Campbell, Miriam Kumaradoss, Janet Matthews, Rosemary Santarelli, Devyn White and Ben Rosenthal. My post thesis ladies work shoppers: Afia, Janet and Rosemary for graciously sharing your talent. I love you all.

Fellow Columbia writers: Hyatt Bass, David Bradley, Rachel Chait, Louis Elliott, Fernanda Hong, Umair Kazi, Erin Kindig, Geeta Tewari for your above and beyond efforts on my behalf, and my dear friend Seema Srivastava for your love and endless support. For Julian Sharifi for not only reading but enthusiastically asking over and over for new material. And writer Amelia Blanquera, I will miss you forever. Pascale Gousseland PhD. for lighting the self-confidence spark within me and for your friendship. My story-telling family for their inspiration, love and encouragement even while reading the rough stuff: Rita and Dave Holzbaur and Joanie Gawrylowicz. Helen McMahon, Nora McMahon and Edna Morris, for all the memories you shared that fueled my creative juices.

My sister, Ellen Bilangi who demanded to read the nearly finished draft and graciously applauded when she came to the end. My daughter, Liza Engberg for listening to me read this work for hours on end and my son, Nic Iraci for his guidance on the computer and for his insightful creative suggestions.

Michael Stringer, publisher of Fat Dog Books for believing in my work.

Most especially to my husband Joe Iraci for his tireless support, love and patience throughout this endeavor. This book was made possible from inception to completion because of him.

I will always be grateful to everyone who helped me change the trajectory of my life in order to pursue my dream of becoming a writer.

PART ONE

Chapter One

There were the times when my father, drunk, asleep on the sofa would forget to alarm the house. His drunkenness was all too obvious. His breathing was noisy, rowdy even. It echoed his previous night's activity and sounded urgent, had a kind of desperation to it, like he was running away from his last breath. He was hard to rouse and seemed unaware of life going on around him. I could slip out then, sit on the moonlit shoreline and hand feed leftover scraps to raccoons. It was on one of those nights when I heard a voice through the trees.

"They carry rabies, you know? You really shouldn't be hand feeding those raccoons; you shouldn't be near them at all."

Jude was his name. His black wavy hair brushed his shoulders and he had deep blue eyes, they matched his denim jacket. He had a heart-stopping smile, sideways and shy. He was dreamy and with the mist coming in off of the lake, he could have been a dream.

We met whenever we could; Jude eventually warmed up to the raccoons, lost his fear of a rabid attack and joined me in the hand-to-paw feasting. He came alone at first, scouted out the area for the friends who would arrive later. Four guys dressed in black, rowed up to my shoreline. They would look at me suspiciously, but not once did they talk to me. They smoked weed and passed around bottles hidden in paper bags before rowing back to wherever they came from. The raccoons stayed away, out of sight as if they intuited a sense of something sinister in the air. Jude stayed behind.

"Your friends seem so much older than you."

"They were friends of my older brother. He died of an overdose last year. He was only twenty-three, six years older than me. His friends let me hang out with them. I guess it makes them feel better about things."

"I'm sorry about your brother." Jude didn't answer, instead he said something I thought was an odd response, especially for someone who had lost a relative to drugs.

"There's money in selling this." He was holding up a lit joint. "It'll be legal everywhere soon. We could do well if we get a head start on everyone else. You know, together."

I shook my head even though when he said the word, *together,* it made me feel special. But I knew I couldn't give in.

"Nothing good will come of this Jude, you'll get caught or get caught up. Do something better with your life. Don't make it bad." I laughed referring to the Beatles song but Jude didn't get the reference.

"What about you? Your life isn't so great."

I had confided in him, told him more than I should have. It was what loneliness did, made you talk to the first person who was willing to listen.

"I don't know you very well and I don't know your parents but they've suffered one loss and probably couldn't handle another. Don't disappoint them; don't get caught up in this life."

Jude touched my arm and a warm, tingly feeling surged through me. He leaned in close but I backed away. He was cute and it made it hard to resist. I had enough problems. I couldn't save myself, how could I save him?

"How old are you anyway? You seem to have life figured out, not your own though. C'mon let me take you away from here. We could go anywhere; I have some cash from dealing."

"I can't, that would make me a cliché."

"What does that mean?"

I didn't answer him. If I went with him, ventured Bonnie and Clyde like into that world, I would be the classic girl from a bad situation following the wrong path, as expected. Cliché! It was the end, Jude got into his boat and sailed up the lake and out of sight.

It was morning, yet last night's rain still dotted the windowpane like spent tears. A strong breeze struggled to make its way through the three-inch opening of the alarmed sill. Raising it any higher would cause a shrill sound to flood the lakefront, the trees to shake as the birds flew off and raccoons to stand upright in their tracks taking notice with ears raised in unison.

It was only my mother, Meghan, home now, pretending to be working but really spending hour after uneasy hour trying to figure out what to do with me. She's always antsy. We're alarmed in because she has suburban phobia. Lakeside living conjures up images in her head of escaped convicts hiding out from the authorities, holding innocents hostage. She preferred city life, where in her mind, everyone was safe, defended to the death by round the clock doormen. I'd never been a part of her city life; she kept me hidden from her society friends. Her time at home in the past, before she kicked my father to the curb, added up to days not years. My childhood memories of her are nil. The alarm was always set now, keeping intruders out and me trapped inside, not alone, but lonely still.

My mother never wanted kids. I heard her say it to her phantom friend, Maggie on the phone. Or maybe it was a wish she'd made out loud when she knew I was in earshot. She did tell me once, I was merely a comma on a page in the book of her life, a pause, a mere blip. But, her mean streak wasn't always showing. We used to engage in brief, once in a while talks on the phone from some faraway place where she was conducting business. She left me then, semi-permanently in the care of my stay-at-home father. She seldom returned, but when she did, she breezed in and out again a few days later. You wouldn't call us a family, we were more like passengers adrift on the same boat, floating away in different directions.

When I was small, my father called his business, *the don't tell your mother game.* Now Meghan was the one here and she had little to say to me so it was a surprise to see her at the door to my room.

"Jenna, we need to talk," she said with a shaky voice. She walked in without knocking and fiddled with the hairbrush on my dresser. She spoke with her back to me.

"I need to go away on business, will you be okay here by yourself?" She didn't wait for an answer. What difference did it make? I was alone most of the time anyway. It was summer and there wouldn't be a tutor coming until the fall. I was seventeen now, too old for nannies and baby sitters.

My father never liked strangers in the house so it was odd he wanted me to be home-schooled. I had been in school when I was younger; the only thing I remembered was the school had been shut down. My father was gone now. He vaporized along with Jude. I had nothing but my books to distract me for the next few months.

A limo driver appeared at the door and took my mother's four bags. It seemed like a lot of luggage for a business trip. I walked her to the door where she regaled me with a litany of uncharacteristic motherly instructions: "Do not open the door under any circumstances; I left money in case of emergency but I don't expect anything to happen. There's plenty of food. I'm not expecting any packages and the mailman will throw the mail through the slot in the door. You are not to talk to anyone. Don't open the door to anyone either. The cameras are on. Is all this clear?" She was talking into the mirror in the hall, puffing up her flat blonde hair with one hand and smoothing out her lipstick with the other.

"Sure Mom," I said, knowing she hated to be called mom. What else was new? I never went anywhere, where would I go now? One camera or another had always been focused in my direction.

"When I get back, we'll go shopping, get you some new clothes, do something about your hair; you'd like that wouldn't you?" She fluffed up the hair on one side of my head and made a face. I nodded, knowing whatever she was saying would never happen. "Maybe even find a proper school for you to go to," she added.

After all this time, being out of a traditional school, she wanted me to start attending high school in my final year. The possibility of this reality on my horizon was just one more thing for me to stress over. I barely remembered school; I was so young when the school closed suddenly. No one ever mentioned it again. I stayed home after that, but I always wondered if my father had something to do with it.

"Oh, and Jenna, call me Meghan; we use names not titles, remember?"

She gave me air kisses on both sides of my cheeks and in a voice full of faux tears said, "I wish I could take you with me but you'd be so bored. I'll be in meetings day and night. It's better this way. I'll be back as soon as I can."

She didn't say when that would be and I could almost see the air of indifference clinging to her designer suit as she blasted out the door. She covered her phone with one hand and yelled to me out the window, "I almost forgot, Alan is coming by. He needs some camera equipment he left behind. I think he said, on Friday but I'm not sure, doesn't matter."

The limo sped up the road and faded from view. For a moment, I wondered if she had a boyfriend. I closed the door and locked it. I felt panic rise up into my throat. Suddenly, I was cold and clammy. Alan was coming back; I couldn't see him, I won't. Being ignored was preferable to being exposed by him.

Chapter Two

I spent the first day alone reading: *The Complete Poems of Emily Dickinson.* My tutor, Miss Melnyk, had assigned it to me and then gave it to me as a present. She was a nice lady with a slight Ukrainian accent. She gave me generous hugs and always asked me how I was doing. Maybe this was a normal greeting between a tutor and a student, but my father's eyebrows would lower whenever she asked. He feared I would reveal the truth. She noticed his sneer. I could tell she was afraid of him. Her words turned to whispers whenever he came near. She was probably here illegally and I'd bet she knew her days were numbered. I'd probably never see her again.

I was almost halfway through the seven-hundred and twenty pages of the book. Emily Dickinson appealed to me with her white dress and clear sense of self. I didn't know who I was, not really. I imagined myself someday dressed all in white, perched up high where I could send baked goods in a basket tied to a rope down to neighborhood children who waited below. I too, would write secret thoughts, hide them in poetic verse for some future scholar to find and figure out. They would be published long after I died and then everyone would know and maybe be sorry.

Analyzing Emily's poetry was tiring. I fanned the pages of the large book and noticed scribble next to the poem: *Down Time's Quaint Stream*…it was a note from Miss Melnyk, *Remember Jenna, your life belongs to you. Study this poem, memorize it and choose your own path.* No, I thought, I would not be seeing Miss Melnyk again.

"Choose my own path?" I said out loud. How? My whole world existed inside this house now. I had one chance to leave and I'd blown it. What choices would I have now? There was a whole world out there, I read about it. I saw kids my age in movies and on T.V. I knew how they talked and how they stood up to their parents. I read but I couldn't absorb it all. I listened to Jude and his friends talk about stuff I couldn't relate to. I knew I wasn't meant for this life; I was meant for something else. I felt it. My mind was racing with thoughts of escape.

The sun was going down over the lake outside the back of the house. I listened as the loons crowed a nightly song. It sounded like they were laughing as they flew off of the lake and into the trees. Laughing at me, the human girl caged while they flew free. I turned on the TV for company and then all the lights. I was not afraid, I told myself. I looked out the window and willed Jude to appear. When he didn't, Miss Melnyk's words echoed in my head.

On the second day of my solo living, I ventured into my mother's room. I figured if I put everything back in its place I could snoop around. Her closet floor was covered with papers. I pushed them aside and pulled out the cardboard box tucked behind the pile. Inside was an address book and a small manila envelope labeled: *Jenna's P.P.* I opened it slowly, and inside was a small blue booklet. I closed it fast and put it back. Why would my mother get me a passport? Was she planning on taking me away or sending me away?

A passport? I could leave here; I could go anywhere if I had enough money. Meghan hadn't called; who knew when she'd be back or if she was coming back at all? Where could I go? My mind was still racing; I opened the address book and looked at the unrecognizable names. Most were business acquaintances but there in the O's was the name: Katherine O'Connor 2211 Broadway, New York, New York. Who was this? My mother once told me all her relatives were dead. I remembered it clearly, *I'm the last of my tribe,* she said without flinching. Maybe this was a cousin.

In the back of the closet was another metal box. Inside was Meghan's birth certificate: *Meghan O'Connor born-New York City-Mother: Katherine Daly O'Connor; Father: Michael O'Connor.* I put it back quickly and felt my face redden. No one was here but I felt a presence like I was being watched. I had a grandmother, a grandmother I knew nothing about.

When the mood struck her or the moon was full, Meghan would tell me about her childhood in New York. She told me her parents were both dead. Alan never mentioned his family at all. He never told me a story or even read a book to me. I was his commodity, nothing else.

On the morning of the third day, while in the kitchen pouring stale cereal into a bowl and noticing the dishes piling up in the sink, I heard a swish of mail pass through the mail slot in the front door. In a pile were the usual: a bill from Verizon with its signature red and white lettering laying on top along with flyers from ShopRite announcing the sales for the upcoming week. I thought of leaving everything there so when Meghan finally returned she'd have to shovel her way in. I had five days left before I had to deal with my father. I shuddered the thought away and sat by the window overlooking the lake. Under any other circumstances this place would have been considered peaceful.

By Monday afternoon, the mail had invaded most of the entryway. I stepped over it on my way to the kitchen. By Tuesday afternoon, it had spread like a virus and was covering the floor forming a paper rug. By Wednesday, I had no choice but to walk on it all. My bare foot came down hard on a heavy envelope. I picked it up and placed it on a kitchen chair. The "plenty of food" promised by Meghan wouldn't feed an anorexic. I made myself some toast and pulled out a chair from the table knocking the envelope to the floor. I left it there and grabbed some juice. The phone rang and distracted me. I slipped on the envelope and landed on the floor next to it. It was addressed to Meghan O'Connor, she never used her married name: Rose. It was from American Express. I looked around the room and over my shoulder before I tore open the envelope. Inside was a shiny new credit card, Platinum no less. I mulled over the pros and cons of confiscating Meghan's card. Was it stealing if you took your own mother's stuff? I could almost hear her reaction, *put her in a home for troubled girls,* she'd tell the arresting officer. Would this really be so bad? Problems solved all around—Meghan would get rid of me and I'd get to leave here and be with people my own age. It looked adventurous on Lifetime.

Be brave, I told myself as I dialed the 1-800 number and heard the recording. Snag-*type in the last four digits of your social security number.* It had to be here somewhere. Think, Jenna. I'd already ransacked Meghan's closet. The desk in the spare room beckoned; it seemed to be on my side, *get yourself out of here,* it said in my head. While sitting down on the desk chair, I bumped my knee on the file cabinet underneath. Snag: locked-damn! Meghan was too lazy to think of creative hiding places. Time was running out. I looked around and there in plain sight was the key, sitting pretty in the desk drawer, just begging to be used.

In the I-file under income tax was the latest copy of Meghan's tax return. Her social security number was right there on the front page. I had to use it, pretend to be Meghan. But who would want to be Meghan? This was just a temporary necessity, a prerequisite to my escape to freedom.

Your card is activated, a mechanical voice announced. I took the card to the computer and checked the flights out of San Francisco to New York on Expedia. American Airlines: non-stop flight from San Francisco to New York's J.F.K International Airport-First Class: Why not? $1498.10, it was now or never; I had to leave before my father came home.

Tapping my finger a few times on the desk calmed my nerves. I moved it slowly back to the keyboard and pushed submit. The boarding pass was printing. The plane left tomorrow night at 10:55p.m. Better to leave under cover of darkness was a line I'd heard in the movies.

Rebellious defiance and mutinous aspirations imagined for a lifetime bubbled up propelling me forward. A deluge of hostility seemed to erase my fear. I took another look at the lake. It was still and peaceful but there was no sailboat bearing another prince coming again to offer me a life elsewhere. It was up to me to find my own way. Jude had moved on, perhaps to a life of crime, but really, who was I to talk?

Chapter Three

The airport was 100 miles away from Clear Lake. *Lake County Limo Service* was my mother's go to company. They picked her up and dropped her off regularly. The teenager who answered the phone was distracted. I could hear her turning the pages of a magazine. I put on my best Meghan voice and said, "This is Meghan O'Connor, I need a car to pick up my daughter, Jenna, tomorrow evening let's say around six to be on the safe side and drive her to the airport in San Francisco. She'll give you the flight information when you arrive. Thanks, put the charges on my account; oh, and one more thing, send an experienced driver."

"Yes, Ms. O'Connor," the girl said, adding, "all booked, our driver will pick your daughter up at your home address on Sulphur Mine Road, is this correct?"

"Yes, that's right."

"Okay, confirmed," she said on the other end. I breathed out, my hands were soaked and a strange heat was rising up from my neck. I had to calm down so I didn't screw up.

The security cameras outside were connected to the fuse box in the garage. When I turned off the power the phone rang. *Don't panic,* I told myself. The caller ID said, *All County Alarm Co.* I took in a deep breath before I answered, "Hello, yes, I'm using the iron and my sister is vacuuming and a fuse blew; everything is okay here. My name? Oh, it's Meghan O'Connor. Code? Oh yeah, it's Cooper. Thank you, bye."

Good thing, I'd overheard Alan give the code. He used the name of a dog he had when he was a kid. I couldn't imagine him as a kid with a dog. I leaned against the wall; I slid down and sat on the floor and began to wonder if this was going to work. It had to.

For shits and giggles, I took six inches off of my hair, the hair my mother hated. I left dark curly clumps of it on top of the dirty dishes piled in the sink. In case they put an APB out on me, I wouldn't look like who they were looking for; if anyone bothered to look. Revenge was feeling sweet. I felt a wave of release, but I was not there yet. I packed up some summer clothes in the one suitcase which Meghan had left behind. My pasty white face was concealed, dusted with the bronzer I found on Meghan's sink. I threw it in the suitcase. Shorts, a tee shirt and sneakers completed the illusion. I thought I looked like every other kid who was going to visit grandma for the summer. When I caught a glimpse of myself in the mirror, I seemed costumed, creepy and unrecognizable.

The limo arrived twenty minutes early but I was ready. My suitcase was already on the edge of the porch. I didn't want to risk being peppered with intrusive questions like, *Are you home alone?* They already knew my mother's away; they were the ones who had taken her. Still I was not taking any chances.

"Bye Dad, I'll miss you; hope you feel better. I'll call when I land; love you," I yelled through the front door into the empty house. Maybe I should re-route myself to Hollywood. I pulled some courage up from inside my socks and made my way to the car. I turned to look at home, not so sweet home, for what I hoped was the last time. It looked sad and shabby, *don't leave me,* it seemed to say.

Distress Sale, was what they called it when my parents bought it. At least that was the story they told. The previous owner had died and his out of town descendants wouldn't make the trip west to accurately assess its worth, which wasn't much as it turned out. Seventeen years later, the leftover indestructible brown plaid sofa and the token lake house recliner remained in aged splendor in front of the newly added flat screen television. My room was the only other update. It had been decorated regularly, but always with a pink décor.

Pretty in pink, Alan would say laughing. Meghan reserved her decorating talent for her office and the apartment she kept in town to use on the nights she worked late. The office was state of art with its soft leather seating in the waiting room and the imposing glass desk which showed little sign of taxing, laborious mental gymnastics taking place at it. I was there only once; it was pristine and paperless. I'd never seen her apartment.

The closest neighbor we had was a Mrs. Kane. The UPS man called her name several times a week, *Mrs. Kane, here's another package for you from Publisher's Clearing House; hoping to win a bundle huh?* I could always hear the echo of him laughing through the small opening in my window. Sometimes, Mrs. Kane would one finger wave to me from her neighboring deck. With her other hand, she would routinely finger her close-cropped, orangey-red curly hair. I could never tell what color her eyes were. From my vantage point, I imagined them to be a smoky brown, any other color would be clownish, I remember thinking at the time. Now as I was leaving, I thought about what she would say if my story got out, *My, my,* I imagined her saying into the waiting media microphones, *I thought you people were the folks from the Publisher's Clearing House prize patrol. What did you say? A photographer was taking nasty pictures of his own daughter right here next door to me; why I can't believe it.* The thought was chilling.

I asked the driver to wait while I walked around back to the lakefront to take a last look at the raccoons. I heard a commotion on the shoreline; Jude and his friends were back. The sky was suddenly dark and cloudy, I didn't need to see them to know what they were doing.

The limo beckoned, the driver held the door but I told him, "Hang on, I forgot something." I went back inside the house, hesitated a moment, inhaled hard and picked up the phone, *Lake County Police Department,* a female voice answered, *Officer Mullin, can I help you?*

"Hello, yes, I live on the upper end of Sulphur Mine Road. Yes, well there seems to be some teenagers sitting on the shoreline here drinking and doing God knows what else. You'd better send someone out. Oh, my name, is that important? Okay, it's Mrs. Meghan Rose."

Maybe I could save both of us, Jude and I, but I knew deep down I'd never find out for sure. The limo drove slowly down the winding road; a police car sped silently by us with its lights flashing. Jude and his friends wouldn't hear it coming. I felt a sudden chill come over me, I reached into my carryon and grabbed a sweatshirt.

Chapter Four

At 8:45 p.m., the limo pulled up to the curb of the American Airlines departing flights entrance. *Take deep breaths.* I looked around, I wasn't sure for what; no one knew I was here. I checked my bag at the curb along with twenty or so other people; a family of six was ahead of me, I stood close to them trying to blend in. The youngest, a boy of about three started screaming for no apparent reason. The baggage check in guy, unnerved by the whole scene, rushed the family through and me along with them. He barely glanced at my ticket.

Security was next. I cut the long line and followed the roped off area reserved for first class passengers. I wiped my hands on the side of my shorts before presenting the envelope containing my passport and boarding pass to the waiting officer. He read the outside first and turned to his co-worker laughing, "Look at this, just like a kid to hand this to me," I guess it was the *Jenna's P.P.* that struck him funny. My face was flushing; I had to calm down. He took several long looks at the passport and then up at me. *Breathe, let it out; don't tense up.*

"Well, young lady," I stood stiff with fear, stared at him-a stunned deer in the middle of a dark road, "seems like you'll be needing a new passport soon, this one is almost five years old." He handed it back to me, smiling and added, "have a nice trip. Next."

I was the only kid in first class. I sat with other people's parents traveling on business, or on their way home to be with their own kids. The sun had set in more ways than one. I looked out the window at the lights glittering over the fading California landscape. No one sat next to me. The flight attendant, Missy, was attentive at first. Missy seemed an odd name for a forty-something year old woman.

"*Come here, Missy.*" I imagined calling a dog or hearing Meghan say, *listen here, Missy, just what were you thinking stealing my credit card and running away to New York?* Imagining someone named Missy, commandeering a group of frightened passengers floating along in lifeboats after the plane went down was a crazy scene even a fucked-up head like mine couldn't dream up.

"Everything okay over here?" she asked handing me the ginger ale I'd asked for thirty minutes before. "Yeah," I snapped out of my Missy creation and turned on the in-flight movie. It was Kevin Costner starring in, *Black or White,* the story of a kid everyone wanted, unlike me, the story of a kid no one wanted. Depressing!

"Breakfast, breakfast," I opened my eyes to find Missy grinning at me and holding a tray full of mock breakfast. I wasn't hungry, I took the mostly green banana off of the tray and waved the rest away. I was nauseated. What if my grandmother wasn't home? Where would I go? What if she didn't let me in? What if she didn't believe me? What if she thought I was a *Six Degrees of Separation*-type scam artist? What if she was senile? The pilot blared into the overhead speaker interrupting my latest imagined worst-case scenario.

"Blah, blah, we're making our initial descent into JFK International Airport. We should be on the ground in twenty minutes."

The view from my window was surreal; the buildings below stood like impressive, massive, unmatched blocks of concrete that had fallen out of the sky and had landed uncomfortably alongside each other. I was here in New York City. I did it!

Behind me a group of people formed one huge bulk and pushed in unison, me along with them, towards the baggage claim area. *Got the luggage, now what?* I looked around at several warning signs: *Don't get in a car with an unidentified person!* Great, more fear fuel. I saw the airport concierge in the distance.

"Excuse me, what's the easiest way to get to Manhattan from here on public transportation?" I adjusted my voice attempting to sound sophisticated.

"Where you going?"

"Oh, um West 79th and Broadway."

"Not too shabby," he said back. I checked my fear and put on fake hostility. "So, are you going to tell me how to get there or not?"

"Okay, okay! If money is no object, you can take a car service. But cheap and quick, your best bet is the Air-Tran. Get off at Jamaica Station, then switch to either the Long Island Railroad or take the E to Penn Station on West 33rd Street. Then walk north to 34th and east to Broadway, then take the 1 subway to 79th. Piece of cake!" I wrote it all down as fast as I could keep up.

"Thank you, I think."

Since all I had was the hundred-dollar emergency money Meghan left me, I turned to look for the cheap way out. Just then the concierge guy appeared and tapped me on the shoulder. I jumped back, scared. He gave me a pensive look. A long silence hung in the air; *could he sense the truth about me? Don't lose it now, Jenna.*

"What?"

"Oh, sorry, I forgot to tell you, you'll need a Metro-card for the subways," he pointed toward a machine and walked back to his desk, shaking his head from side to side while he muttered something about tourists. *Please accept Amex,* I told the vending machine containing Metro-cards.

"Yay," I yelled out while I slid Meghan's card in and entered the zip code of my former California address. A golden yellow Metro-card dropped into the slot at the bottom of the machine. I grabbed it and tossed the receipt in my bag in case I wanted to pay Meghan back someday. *No, she owed me;* I tossed it in the trash.

The Air-Tran was like something out of a space movie. It was sleek and fast. I splurged and took the Long Island Railroad. The train appeared out of nowhere as if on cue, like a genie summoned from a lamp. This was easier than I thought it would be. An hour later, I was in Manhattan.

Penn Station, instead of being the landmark I'd imagined, was drab and filled with shady looking characters. I rushed up the stairs and toward the exit. The New York City summer air reached out to touch me. The furnace-like heat felt like the atmosphere of another planet. Not that I missed it, but Clear Lake was just like its name, almost see through, with crisp, clean air hovering over it. Meghan thought it was a refuge, not sure why since she was rarely there. It was never my refuge.

People were hurrying about, like they were running the *Amazing Race*. I heard someone call out *Jude*, I turned around to see a little boy running ahead of his mother. The noise on the street was bordering on unbearable, speaking in one thunderous voice, assaulting all five of my senses at once, making it hard for me to concentrate on where I was going, but at the same time, taking my mind off my other worries. What did the airport guy say? I looked at my notes. One block north, but which way was north? One block to the east, I looked to my right-32nd Street, okay turn left. Dragging this suitcase over the cracked sidewalk was challenging. I'd been working hard since the inception of this plan; I took a risk, now all I needed was pure luck. And also, a change of attitude; I decided to expect something wonderful to happen on the other side of this journey. But then I arrived at the steps of the uptown subway; they seemed daunting, dark and ominous. I pioneered myself this far, I was almost there, too late to wimp out.

PART TWO

Chapter One

The subway station had a musty smell. To me, it resembled a catacomb without relics. The two-block walk in the fiery heat felt like a heavy blanket was draped over me. But now, the roar of the train and the swish of the air from its wake seemed to pump adrenaline through my veins. The cool stale air of the station had the same artificial quality as the heat up above. I stepped into the open door of the 1 train with the ease of a New York commuter. The train lingered as if it too was suffering from the same heat lethargy as the rest of the city. Somehow, I felt secure inside the belly of the subway car. I imagined myself, a subterranean child, an *Eloise* of the subway scene. Forty-five blocks were erased and I was back on the street. I readjusted my eyes to the still morning summer light and did a full spin to get my bearings. There across the street was my grandmother's apartment building. Inert, I stood on the curb, unable to move my leaden feet. What if she didn't know me; didn't believe I was who I said I was? Then what? I came this far. I took baby steps to the driveway at the entrance of the building and spilled into the lobby with most of my worldly goods in tow.

"May I help you?" *If only*, I thought. The doorman ran by me to move my bag out of the doorway.

"12H, Mrs. Katherine O'Connor, please."

"Is she expecting you?"

"I don't think so but I'm her granddaughter, Jenna Rose." He picked up the phone and spoke Spanish to whomever was answering.

"Si, okay... I mean they say it's okay."

"They do?" *Don't these people watch Law and Order?* Anyone could say they were anyone and get in anywhere at any time. I should know, I was a master.

The elevator stopped on 12; the door to 12 H was ajar. I knocked softly, then pushed the door open and walked in. I felt odd, like I was out of my body. My sneakers went into a skid and I slid across the marble floor losing my balance. Grabbing onto a table in the foyer kept me from landing on my ass but I left fingerprints on the mahogany. Grandmother appeared suddenly, took my arm and placed me onto the lap of a soft white leather chair in her living room.

She appeared younger than the seventy-something she was. Her hair looked like it had once been a chestnut color but now had faded with age, leaving bits of grey streaking through it. It was cut short and fell just above her shoulders. I felt better and stood up nervously. My eyebrows raised themselves when I realized I was taller than she was.

"So, you are Jenna? Nice to finally meet you," she said in a calm soft voice. It was like she was expecting me, waiting for my arrival.

"You know about me?"

"Yes, I know about you, but what I don't know is what you're doing here. Where is your mother?"

Grandmother was wearing a neatly pleated, cotton tan skirt, which fell just to her knee. A short-sleeved blouse was tucked in place. Her flat ballet shoes did nothing for her height. I felt messy in her presence. Running my fingers through my hair temporarily loosened the tangles. I tugged on my shorts to make them seem longer, while she studied me with piercing green eyes and asked again, "Why are you here, Jenna?"

"To see you, why else? Can I lie down somewhere, please? I left late last night and I haven't slept." It wasn't the truth; I slept like a hibernating bear on the plane but exhaustion hit me hard now.

Grandmother ushered me down a hall to her best guest room. "I'm sorry this room is such a stark white, like everything else in this apartment. I'm sure at your age you'd prefer a more colorful room."

The room overlooked a tree-lined courtyard. The Hudson River peeked out between the branches. The all-white room was serene in contrast to the creepy Pepto-Bismol pink room of my never-ending childhood.

Grandmother spread her arms wide, pulled me into them and said, "I'm glad you're here, have a rest and come out when you're ready and then we can have a chat, okay?"

She closed the door tenderly. She seemed to touch most things that way as if they would crumble if she pressed any harder. I sat myself down on the window seat and watched the birds watch me while they ate from a feeder perched outside on a small balcony.

The queen-sized white bed beckoned with its feather covers. I fell asleep listening to the exotic city sounds while light beams played on the ceiling. When the door creaked open, I opened my eyes, gasped, pulled up my legs, held them tightly to my chest and shook with fear. I felt disoriented and didn't realize right away where I was. Grandmother was at the door.

"It's only me, I didn't mean to startle you. It's almost dinnertime. Come to the dining room when you're ready."

She closed the door behind her with the same gentle touch. I showered in the white tiled bathroom, lingering under the hot rain coming from the wide showerhead. I waited for a muse to appear, preferably one with enough creative fiction abilities to help me devise a tale of woe to tell my grandmother. What could I say? How could I tell her, *your daughter left me alone with my slimy father for most of my life and she's the anti-mother and my father is a creep of monumental proportions?*

Chapter Two

When the smell of comfort food spread from the kitchen to the guest room, I was unable to resist. I found my way through the apartment to the dining room. It was larger than the lake house or maybe it just seemed this way because it was bright and airy. Grandmother wasn't kidding, the entire apartment was painted white. The white upholstered furniture melted into the white walls but it wasn't stark. It worked, in fact, the walls and the furniture seemed to pose in a decorating magazine like splendor against the dark stained wood floors.

Grandmother was already seated at the too big for two people mahogany table, and a place was set for me. The take-out dinners I was used to didn't require my presence at a table, a place setting or even a dinner companion. Something smelled safe here.

The family pictures on the fireplace mantle caught my attention. There were some of my mother as a kid and none of my father. They spilled over onto a large side table. My mother was an only child. There were no siblings to mix in and diffuse whatever happened between my mother and her parents. Grandmother had a slight aura of sadness around her. I looked over at the largest picture of my mother, a black framed graduation from something, 11x14 glossy. I imagined her looking out with her arrogant stance, out over the camera lens and on toward her neatly planned future. I guessed she was about 18; she oozed confidence as she played with the camera, daring it, telling it, *I don't have a shy bone in my body; I will set the world on fire and no kids for me...ever.* It was all there on her face, how it was going to turn out, she would remain carefree and unencumbered, no matter what.

"That's your mother's high school graduation picture. She looks a bit snobby, doesn't she? It was a snooty high school full of indulged girls. It wasn't my choice to send her there, but well now it's all in the past." Grandmother seemed to be talking more to herself than to me. Before I could answer her, a petite woman in a white uniform with a black apron came in carrying a tray of food.

"Katrina, this is my granddaughter Jenna, she came all by herself from California to see me." "Hello, Miss, nice to meet you. I didn't know you had a granddaughter, Mrs. O'Connor."

Grandmother didn't answer and instead smiled at Katrina, patted her arm and gestured for her to leave the tray.

"Where's Mom, Jenna?"

"You mean Meghan? Mom isn't her thing." Grandmother furrowed her brow and glared at me.

"So, where's Meghan?"

"I don't know, I really don't. She went away on a business trip; she didn't call so I decided to come here."

Grandmother looked at me intently. "I'm trying to figure who it is you favor."

I favored no one. I had skin as pale as day old death and my hair was dark with loose curls; my eyes were like pools of oil. I looked more like a zombie than either of my parents. I was hoping I would look like my grandmother but she had a pinked-up complexion. She returned to the subject of my arrival.

"Where is your father? Isn't he home either?" She didn't know they got divorced; I had to tell her.

"Jenna, did something happen? Please tell me. I will have to try and find your mother. You are under age, you know?"

"They got divorced about four months ago. Alan left in February, haven't seen him since."

"I'm sorry, I didn't know. Your mother and I aren't close. You probably already know that."

"I don't think my mother is close with anyone, not even me."

Grandmother greeted me with, "Good afternoon," when I finally emerged from my room the next day. "Sorry, I never sleep late like this. I must be jet lagged," I said even though I knew it wasn't the truth.

"Breakfast is long over, but there is cereal if you'd rather have that and not lunch, which Katrina is preparing right now."

I couldn't decide if Grandmother's household was routinely regimented or if it was on my account. She seemed nervous; maybe I was disrupting the status quo. Of course, I was, I barged in uninvited and unannounced.

"Grandmother, maybe I should've tried to call you before I came here."

"Jenna, it's perfectly all right. I'm happy you came to see me. But I still need to call your mother at some point, unless you can give me a good reason why I shouldn't."

"I think I'll have some cereal for now, okay?"

The same petite woman, Katrina from the night before brought in an assortment of cereal on a tray along with a pitcher of milk and another of orange juice. She placed it all on the side table in the dining room before returning to the kitchen. A minute later, she returned with a salad for Grandmother. We sat with an anxious hefty silence filling the space between us. Grandmother was the first to talk, "I have some business to attend to today, I cannot cancel. I hate to leave you alone on your first day here but I have to keep this appointment. It's a perfectly safe neighborhood if you want to go out on your own. I won't be late."

"I'll be fine." But what I wanted to say was, *I got myself across the country, I think I can handle the Upper West Side.* I didn't say it though. It was too snarky a comeback for a stuffy grandmother I'd just met. I didn't want to get kicked out on my first full day but still I was proud of myself for finding my own way here.

When Grandmother left, I took myself down to the lobby for a few minutes. Turned out the bravado I'd been experiencing earlier had vaporized now. Panic set in when the doorman opened the door to the big wide city world.

"Oh, sorry I forgot something," I lied.

Katrina finished cleaning up after my breakfast and my grandmother's lunch. "I'll be back later to start dinner," she shouted before heading out the door. Maybe I should latch on to her and let her guide me through the streets until I acclimated myself. Instead, I found my way back to the cozy bed and fell into another deep sleep.

A street lamp came on, shone through the sheer curtains and woke me from a sound sleep. I heard voices from the kitchen, my ear snatched parts of the conversation. "She seems to be healing herself," my grandmother was telling Katrina. "From what, I shudder to think, it's what she's doing; sleep is restorative, it's what she needs now. We have to let her be; she'll tell us when she's ready to."

I stopped listening, *is that what I was doing, healing?* I felt more tired than I'd ever felt before but maybe this was the first time I'd ever been comfortable enough to sleep. I should be uneasy here in this unfamiliar place, but I wasn't at all.

Chapter Three

Three weeks later and Grandmother and I were still doing a dance around each other. She was trying her best not to pry and I was doing my best not to let her. If I had to guess I'd say she was afraid I would run off. I was afraid to tell her my truth, afraid she'd think I was unfit to be her offspring. She didn't bring up calling Meghan so I was surprised to hear her on the phone with her.

"Meghan, it's your mother. Jenna is here with me. She flew here a few weeks ago; I don't know why or how she managed to get here on her own but she did. I'm trying to let her be until she wants to tell me what the problem is. She does seem troubled. I assume you know how you can reach me. Call me when you get back."

There was a gruff tone in her voice I hadn't heard before now. Something bitter hovered in the air. I wondered, for a minute what had happened between these two. Then it occurred to me that whatever it was, it would pale in comparison to what went on in my childhood. When the call ended, I backed myself down the hall and into my room, I faked a yawn for effect while I returned to the hallway as Grandmother was opening her door. Acting was becoming second nature to me.

It took another whole week for Meghan to call back. This time I couldn't hear a word Grandmother was saying and she didn't mention any of it to me. She seemed to be waiting for me to open up, tell her my life story. It was nearly a month since I'd landed on her doorstep. There was a kind of contented restlessness developing between us, I thought. But then the questions started.

"So, did you have a good year at school?" Grandmother asked one morning at breakfast. My mouthful of toast wasn't going down easily. I coughed, then got up to stand at the kitchen sink.

"Are you all right, Jenna?"

"Sure, fine." I thought now she'd forget what she asked, but no, she went right back to it when I sat down.

"So?"

"Oh, I used to go to school, but it closed and now I'm home-schooled. I have tutors, one is really nice."

"Don't you want to go to school? Have friends? Even a boyfriend?" she asked with a smile. I shrugged. No one ever asked me what I wanted before now.

"My father wanted me home, but I have some friends," I lied. The group with Jude on the lake were not friends.

"Why did he want you home?" she asked but stood to get to the phone before I could answer her. I took a deep breath and let it out hard. Katrina entered and eyed me strangely, "You okay, Miss?" I nodded my head, forcing a smile.

When Grandmother returned, she sat back down, keeping her eyes on me. She was about to tell me something and it was as if she wanted to see my immediate reaction to her words. "That was your father, your mother is sending him here to see you and to find out why you ran away. He'll be here on Friday."

Grandmother took her coffee cup and walked toward the kitchen muttering, "It took them long enough to call." Then she told Katrina, "First they claim Meghan thought Jenna was with Alan, and he thought she was with Meghan. Oh, and apparently a neighbor saw a group of kids get arrested by the lake so they looked into the possibility Jenna was with them. Did it even occur to them to listen to their answering machine? Unbelievable!"

I felt flushed and sick to my stomach. My father, why him? Why didn't Meghan ask to talk to me herself? I scrambled to think of something to say to Grandmother. I didn't want to see my father, ever. It was why I came here in the first place. I thought I was home free. I thought I could rebirth myself, and like an amnesiac wipe the slate clean and start over. I followed Grandmother into the kitchen. "Oh no, I forgot to tell you, I met a girl in the building when I was getting the mail the other day. She invited me out on Friday, I can't say no."

I was whining out a pitiful lie. It was only a partial lie because I had seen a girl about my age in the lobby but I hadn't actually met her. Grandmother shot me a pensive look, then she raised her eyebrows as her piercing green eyes seemed to ferret out the lie.

"Okay, we'll see." We'll see what? I wondered but left it alone.

The subject was closed for the time being. "You know, I teach cooking classes? I suppose you noticed I instruct Katrina from time to time and every other day or so a few student cooks come in for a lesson. It's slow in the summer, but in the fall, it will be busy around here. Katrina is taking a few days off now so we'll need to make some dinner plans."

"Can we cook? Please, I never get to, I'd like to learn," I said all in one breath.

"Yes, that would be nice, Jenna," was all she said. I knew she suspected something was terribly wrong with my life. She took one last sip of coffee before putting the cup in the sink. "I need to make a call." After her bedroom door closed, I tiptoed over to it to listen.

"No, sorry Alan, it isn't going to work out this Friday. She isn't going to be here; she has her heart set on being with a girl she's met in my building. She's Jenna's age and I hear Jenna doesn't have many friends. She seems to spend a lot of time alone and is home-schooled. Is this true? I see, so this should be good for her. Yes, of course I know the girl, she comes from a wonderful family and I've already told Jenna she can spend the night and possibly the whole weekend with them. Well, I wish we'd known you were coming east. I know Jenna will be disappointed not to be able to see you and it would have been nice for me to finally meet you."

Grandmother's story telling was flawless and she told her version of my lie with enthusiasm. She spoke eloquently with a convincing voice as soft as a whisper as she expanded on my lie, adding her own fine details. I didn't know why she was lying for me but I was relishing in the thought of Alan having a breakdown over all this.

Chapter Four

The next morning, I got up early to beat the heat. It was cooking day and I'd be doing it all. It was exciting, this new freedom of mine. I walked a few blocks north to Zabars. Once, when Meghan felt like talking she mentioned Zabars, as being the best place for bread when she was a kid. After Zabars, my next stop would be Citarella on Amsterdam. Grandmother had given me a pocket-sized map of the city streets, but I didn't want to look like a tourist; I would rather get lost and find my own way. She warned me about using the cell phone on the street but everyone seemed to be holding one. It was liberating walking on the streets with all these people I didn't know and probably would never know. It was early, I was not in a hurry but I felt out of place and tried walking faster to keep up, but keep up with whom I thought, and slowed down. I needed to notice things, keep track of where I was so I could find my way back and eventually become a regular. But for now, I was Gretel, motherless and lost in the woods. I was secretly worried Grandmother would turn out to be sinister.

Zabars, it turned out, had more than bread. Since my mother was a kid, it had grown into a gourmet fairyland. There were at least fifteen kinds of bread and cheeses with names I couldn't pronounce. I settled on a simple loaf of raisin bread. A man behind the counter handed me a sample of unasked for Camembert cheese. I added a half a pound to the order.

When I first walked in, the cool air of Citarella hit me along with a spray of water meant for the vegetables lining the aisle. I grabbed some carrots and shyly ordered four chicken cutlets from the butcher. I followed the narrow one-way path around the store to the checkout, paid and made my way home. It felt odd calling Grandmother's apartment home. Bits and pieces of sadness lingered around me; it was all holding on tight and hard to shake free. But the sun was out and the city was so distracting. Taking it all in I felt energized and free. It felt like my first day on the planet.

A woman passed by me wearing a fur coat and a velvet hat. She had white gloves on each hand that crept up under her coat. It was just as crazy to see someone in a coat and gloves in the heat of summer, as it was to see the man to the right of her shuffling through the chained garbage cans.

I'd barely walked five blocks when the city heat put that same heavy blanket over me. It was a fiery, inescapable heat beating down on the concrete sidewalks. I made it to 86th and Broadway and spied the subway. I braved it again. I tucked my sweat soaked hair into a ponytail and shoved it under my baseball cap. I took off my sunglasses before I descended, once again, into the underworld. I slid my Metro-card into the slot and waited on the platform for the arriving 1 train. Seven blocks swished by and I was back on the street. I readjusted my eyes to the harsh light and did my usual spin around to get my bearings. I saw him before he saw me.

Chapter Five

I put my sunglasses back on and pulled the front of my hat down over my eyebrows. I felt a different kind of heat come over me. My father was walking on the opposite side of Broadway with a woman so blonde she seemed translucent. His camera was dangling from a cord around his neck. He had his arm cozily around the woman and with his left hand he was pulling a girl from behind. She was dragging her feet; she was young, about ten or eleven. She seemed to be more substantial than her mother; she was less blonde, less wispy and probably capable of walking away, running, screaming, anything. But she was trapped and tethered. I shared her uneasiness.

He came here anyway, probably was here already when Grandmother called him. He was doing it again, or still. He found someone else, a replacement me, a younger version. Did I even care? I was free now. I found a safe harbor, but it still felt like I'd been cast away.

My heart raced as my feet kept going without me toward Grandmother's building. I willed him not to see me. I couldn't seem to breathe. Panic was lodging itself in my throat. I couldn't lose control; I wouldn't. Once beyond the doorman, I'd be safe; no one got through unannounced. I was a regular now, I belonged.

The northbound bus stopped and was blocking my view. I lost sight of them for a minute. The light changed, the bus hesitated in the crosswalk, then reopened its door and graciously allowed a latecomer to enter. I watched with eyes to the left and used the added time to cross over 79th Street and then made headway to the building. The trio missed the light; the woman eased my father's arm off of her shoulder, grabbed the child by her wrist and shook her firmly. I kept my head riveted toward the street while my body found the lobby. I heard my father yell, "Jenna" over the din of traffic.

"We're not home if anyone comes by," I heard a disembodied voice tell the doorman. It took a few seconds for me to realize I was the one who was talking. I knew this was one of the perks of a doorman building; my grandmother had told me. Now it was my armor. The doorman was my unwitting prince, my super hero. I let my mind wander to my less empowered days as I pushed the gold button too many times and tripped into the empty elevator. It closed its door like a valve cocooning me in its metal womb. I collapsed onto the floor and leaned against the back wall of the elevator. I dropped my head to my knees. I was shaking but wasn't going to cry. I was safe, for now. I'd created my own security in strange places, the acrid subway, an elevator and in the home of a grandmother I barely knew. I felt a jolt in my stomach and as the elevator began to move, I heard it say, "You see a ghost, or something?" I looked up and slid myself against the back wall of the elevator and raised myself to my feet. There, in the corner, was the girl I'd seen weeks before. She was about my age, maybe older, tall and thin. She was wearing blackout sunglasses with rimless frames. She pushed the sunglasses up like a makeshift headband to the top of her head, sliding her silky black hair along with them and looked me over from top to bottom. An unlit cigarette dangled defiantly from the corner of her mouth. She placed herself, intentionally, no doubt, underneath the *No Smoking* sign. I liked her already.

The elevator opened on seven and let a suit in. The suit was all I saw. It made a fist and slammed the L button with three consecutive side punches willing it to change direction. The elevator climbed skyward ignoring the suit's attempt to derail our destination. The girl ignored the suit and pulled her sunglasses back over her eyes taking the, *if I don't see you, then you don't see me,* approach, and joined me at the back of the elevator. The suit took her place in the front corner, tapped his foot impatiently and fixed his eyes on the rising numbers over the elevator door.

"Well, did you?" The girl asked revealing for the first time her slightly gapped front teeth.

"Did I what?"

"See a ghost?"

"No, just my father."

The elevator stopped on ten and she put her foot in the doorway holding it open. "Well are you coming or not?"

"Uh, I have groceries, I have to cook for my grandmother."

"It's barely noon. It's even too early for the early bird special. She a hundred? C'mon, you can put the groceries in Adele's fridge. She won't be home for days." The suit let out a sigh. I followed the girl down the hallway.

"Who's Adele?"

"Oh, her, she's my mother. I'm Gabrielle, by the way, but you can call me, Gypsy, everyone does," she said extending her hand.

"I'm Jenna, here from California, living with my grandmother now. You call your mother by her first name; it's funny because I do too. Mine, I mean." I shook my head to clear it. "I call my mother by her first name too."

"Mom cramps Adele's style." Gypsy rolled her eyes. I nodded nervously. She works for a magazine, it's not exactly mommy central." I could have related to this but instead of commenting I asked, "Where did you get the name, Gypsy?"

"My full name is Gabrielle Yvonne Puteri; get it? GYP? It just turned into Gypsy. My father used to call me, *Princess,* it's what Puteri means in Malay. He's Malaysian. They're divorced, he and Adele.

"Yeah, mine too, divorced I mean. My father called me, *Princess,* too once." I looked away. "I didn't like it, but he didn't care. I call my mother, Meghan, it seems to perpetuate the differences between us."

"Does everyone in California talk like you?"

"I don't know."

Gypsy raised an eyebrow at me. She probably thought I was just released from an institution.

"But I thought that was where you were from?

"I am, but I was home-schooled and I didn't have many friends. I read a lot. We lived far from civilization so I got books from Amazon. I looked up words I didn't know." I was sounding strange even to myself.

Gypsy furrowed her brow again and looked at me narrowing her light brown eyes. They weren't brown exactly, they were a coppery color with tiny flecks of gold. I'd never seen eyes like hers before. I followed her down the hall where the smells of curry and stale cigarette smoke led us to the apartment where Gypsy lived with Adele. It had a courtyard view, different than at Grandmother's, with the disheveled appearance of an unmade bed. Clothes were strewn all over and on chairs in the living room and the dining room table was covered with papers. Gypsy made no apologies for the mess. She put the groceries, bags and all, into the empty fridge.

"Let's go to Riverside Park," Gypsy blurted out.

"I don't want to go back out."

"Ah, c'mon it's a nice day. No one will see you, I promise."

I found myself following her again. She was like an alter ego; an exotic other me I could be if I had the courage. Maybe she'd rub off. I felt a little braver. But she seemed so at ease in the world, so at ease with herself.

We left the apartment and went in the opposite direction of the elevator through a door clearly marked, *Service, Staff Only*; I pointed to the sign. Gypsy shrugged and continued through to a stairwell where commercial buckets and mops were standing by to service the next mishap. Further back was the Service Elevator. We got on and took it down to the basement. It opened to a back driveway where dumpsters and garbage cans were carefully positioned to be concealed from the elitist eyes of the residents.

I followed Gypsy like a lost puppy, toward Riverside Park and down to the boat basin. We took the stone steps to a spot where a fountain sprayed and water pooled underneath it.

"Take off your shoes, it's hot. Let's walk in the water," Gypsy instructed as she kicked off her sandals and climbed over the stone façade. To me, she seemed totally free. I removed my sneakers as instructed and joined her in the fountain. I was nervous and it probably showed. I searched around for my father and his groupies. I was not used to fun; I thought of logistical things.

"How are we going to dry our feet?" Gypsy just stared at me and said nothing. I changed the subject, "What do you do around here all summer?"

"I wait for Wilhelmina to call," she said while looking at her cell phone.

"Who's that, your sister?"

"No, no sister, no brother, no relatives at all other than Adele and my father, wherever he is. But I did have a grandmother once. She died of a heart attack but I think it was a broken heart because her daughter didn't love her." Gypsy looked out over the river.

"But you must have loved her."

"I never met her; Adele wouldn't let me, they had some stupid fight. Everyone needs grandparents and lots of them if you can find people who are willing. You don't have to be blood-related. I think so anyway. Grandparents are a respite from parents. See, New Yorkers know words." Gypsy's eyes filled. For a minute, I thought she was going to cry but she turned around, suddenly cheered up and said, "Wilhelmina's my agent; I'm a model. It's one of the perks of being freakishly tall."

"Wow, cool," I said while Gypsy held her open pack of cigarettes gesturing for me to take one. I shook my head. "I don't smoke."

"You look like you should. You should do something. What's going on with you, anyway? You looked weirded out in the elevator, I know that look. So, what is it?"

"It's nothing, nothing." Now it was my turn to gaze out over the water.

"You don't have to tell me but you should tell someone. Whatever it is. You almost knocked me down in the lobby and you didn't even notice I was in the elevator with you. You've got some serious issues going on girl."

I didn't know how to respond, so we just sat in silence on a bench by the water. I took a drag from her cigarette; I didn't see the great attraction. I gave it back to her and waved my hand in front of my face, coughing and clearing the smoke.

"I better get back." We walked through the park to Riverside Drive and took 82nd Street up to Broadway, which was a sea of people. Gypsy fingered a faux designer bag which was hanging on the side of a street vendor's table.

"This is total crap," she said loud enough for half of the world to hear. "You make this in your basement?"

"Just trying to make a living, now get the hell out of here," the vendor snapped while standing protectively in front of his cart. Gypsy just laughed, while I looked around for signs of my father but he was nowhere in sight. I retrieved the groceries from Adele's fridge.

"Thanks, that was fun. I hope I see you again soon."

"How about later? I'm not doing a thing, we can watch a movie." She had a slight pleading tone in her voice but I didn't want to make any definite plans. She gave me her cell number and I made my way out the door.

Gypsy yelled down the hall after me, "Tell your grandmother, she's cool; kind of like *Yoda*, from *Star Wars."*

"Tell her what?"

"You know." Yes, I knew but how did she know and how did she know my grandmother's cool?"

Chapter Six

I opened the door to Grandmother's apartment and entered as quietly as I could.

"Jenna, is that you? I was starting to worry." *Was it Jenna? I wasn't sure. I'd stepped off the pages of my old, sad story and into a new realm. Was I still the same person? Did I even know how to be a person, my own person? No, I wouldn't think about who I used to be and what was expected of me then, I wouldn't.*

"Yeah, I'm back with the groceries. Should I get started on dinner?" I took out the onions, carrots, chicken and balsamic vinegar marinade from the bag. I sliced the bread into thin pieces and put them on the table with the cheese.

"You smell like cigarettes," Grandmother said while lifting the onion.

"Someone on the street was smoking near me." *I didn't know why I told her that and not about Gypsy. It was something else of my own I didn't want to share just yet.*

Grandmother showed me how chefs cut an onion so it cooked evenly. She held the knife and sliced a few horizontal cuts into the side of the onion. She firmly grasped it with the other hand and made downward cuts before slicing it again crossways. The onion pieces fell like ballet dancers in perfect order onto the cutting board. Grandmother had gone to the *French Culinary Institute* back in the '80s. After that, she practiced her skills expanding my grandfather's waistline. Now she taught cooking in her kitchen, giving the people who work for her a skill. It was more of a hobby than a job.

"It takes practice," she told me. I put the chicken cutlets in a zip-lock and drowned them in the marinade. I emptied the bag of carrots while Grandmother sat down at the dining room table. I sensed she was getting ready to tell me something. I was so afraid she was going to ask me to leave. I stood bone still, not breathing. When I heard her begin to tell a story, I sighed letting out a deep breath.

"I was a displaced kid too, you know? My mother died when I was eight. My father was here and there before he disappeared for good. After that, my aunts stepped in and divvied us five kids up like winnings at a card game."

"Where did you go?" I asked gently while chopping the carrots.

I was not really interested in talking. I listened though since I rarely got to hear anyone tell me about their childhood. Miss Melnyk told me once about growing up in the Ukraine. It was so far removed from my own childhood it seemed like a fairy tale. Grandmother's story was sounding unreal to me too.

"For weeks, after my mother died, I had been visiting my godmother, Aunt Eileen. She had been my mother's best friend. A few days after my father left, I packed up my pajamas, a toothbrush, my hairbrush, my ratty clothes and a whole lot of hope, I guess, into a paper bag I had found under the sink and took myself across Columbus Avenue. It was an unspoken invitation like an opening in a fence, so I just invited myself into her apartment where she lived with her two sisters, Anna and Noreen and her brother, Jimmy who was dying of cancer."

The story flowed like a lazy river as the carrots simmered in butter and sugar slowly taking on the color of syrup. The story was sad, but it soothed me, made me feel connected, somehow. Grandmother and I had more in common than I thought. She pretty much did the same thing I had done, plopped herself in the middle of someone else's life.

"Jimmy smoked out of a hole in his throat." I made a face but Grandmother said, *she got used to it and didn't notice it after a while.*

"Sometimes I would hold his cigarette for him when the cancer spread from his lungs to his bones, making it too hard for him to do it himself. *Who are you again?* He would cough out the words between puffs while covering the hole so he could speak," she went on, "I am nobody, I would tell him. *Everybody is somebody,* he would say."

"Where did your siblings go?"

"My other siblings went in twos to my mother's sisters."

"Where was the apartment?"

"Just north of here, it was called a railroad apartment. I had long creaking floors connecting a hallway that snaked around from room to room. Jimmy's room was at the head of the snake in front of the kitchen. It was meant to be a maid's room, but there wasn't a maid in those days. Nothing got through the gate-covered window, not an intruder, not even the sun. If you could have looked out, you would have seen the fire escape leading down to the alley where four buildings stood in a square and pigeons searched for scraps."

"Jimmy must have liked you, huh, Grandmother?"

"He seemed to, I remember his eyes had the look of already being where he was going next. I asked him why he smoked with a hole in his throat and he told me that *he may as well see it through to the end.*"

Grandmother explained how the household was a mix of the young and the dying and the aging next in line, all waiting around until they found themselves together again. She said with a laugh, "I guess I'm there now too, in heaven's waiting room."

"Everybody is," I said, "What happened next?" The story gripped me.

"One day after school, I came home and Jimmy was gone." Grandmother continued, "has he gone out? I asked Aunt Eileen. All she said was her brother *was gone and he wouldn't be back.* She was a woman so used to grief that the grieving of one barely had time to take root before the grieving of another was on her. She had been the eldest of ten and now seven siblings were lost.

But Jimmy did come back."

"What? How?"

"Well, the coffee table in the living room where I did my homework was moved out and Jimmy was moved in. He lay in a box for three days while the whole neighborhood came in to say goodbye." Grandmother stared into the distance and seemed miles away for a few minutes. I wondered why she was telling me all this.

"I guess you were sad after Jimmy died?" I said not knowing what to say. The story was getting depressing but I barged in on her and I couldn't really tell her to lighten up. So, on she went.

"Aunt Eileen couldn't stand emotional outbursts or attention drawn to her or me or to any of us. I had to go to school whether I was sick or sad. I was on scholarship at the parish school and a heavy recipient of Christian charity. Aunt Eileen wouldn't allow me to be fodder for the nuns who were seeking time off in Purgatory. But they still fawned over me while shunning my advantaged classmates. They combed my messy hair and gave me other kids' cast-off clothes. They gave me religious instruction and by helping me, it was ensured their souls would be saved."

Grandmother's story was a trip down memory lane. At times, I thought she was just reminiscing for old time's sake, talking to herself really, but then I wondered if she was just trying to draw me in so I would talk about myself.

"I never heard of that, bringing the dead back home and keeping them in their own living room. It's creepy."

"That's how they did it in those days. After three days were up, Jimmy was gone for good. They took him away while I was at school. I imagined they tied his coffin to a rope and then let him down easy out the window, sliding him into the church which was conveniently located just across the street. We lived in a steep six-story walk-up. I always wondered about it, but I didn't dare ask. I did stay away from the living room for a long time after. I sat in the long off-white hallway, my beige cocoon, doing homework, blocking everyone's way and avoiding the scent of death which lingered in my mind. All the earlier childhood living room memories were gone. The happy sounds and recollections of Christmases past had been obliterated from my brain. The remnants of unspoken sorrow hung in the air in the living room paving the way for what was to come. I was transparent; no one noticed I was traumatized."

I couldn't relate to the happy sounds of Christmas or childhood living room memories but somehow, despite never having experienced the death of someone, I felt a connection to Jimmy's tragic story. Maybe it was just a connection to my grandmother. Her childhood sounded as fucked up as mine. This was the kind of story which would sell if someone wrote it down. No one wanted to hear about happiness, well, until the end maybe.

As she told me the story of her early life, she expelled the stored-up memories without effort, scraping them off the walls of the apartment which still held the musty smell of my grandfather's after shave. She was handing over to me bits of her past. I was the one who'd carry the diluted version. Perhaps, it would all live another life through my recreation of it. Maybe talking about it was her way of purging the sorrow of her early years. It overwhelmed me; I related but didn't want to. I forced myself to listen in the hope that through her revelations I'd come to terms with my own truths and have the courage to drop the baggage I was carrying around Maybe talking did dilute the burden of it, lessen the load and diminish the stockpile. Or maybe, I just listened to too much television psycho-babble. Grandmother looked over me, stopping her story for a minute. I was at the stove stirring the carrots.

"Aunt Eileen was a great cook. She was a big, huggable bundle of a woman. I still can remember the smell of her caramelized carrots. She made them every Sunday after we got home from the cemetery in Queens where Jimmy was buried alongside my mother and other relatives and friends. It was normal back then to visit the dead regularly. Aunt Eileen would instruct me to *tell Jimmy how school is going.* I felt foolish but did as I was told. I clung like a grateful tick to her for giving me a home. I always thought I stood on fate's shaky terra firma. I never knew when I would be set adrift into the abyss of foster care."

Grandmother sure had a way with words. I suppose I took after her in that respect. I loved words and looked up everything. I wondered about the origin of words and if I could put them all together as well as she did. Maybe tell my story, write it down since I couldn't seem to say it. Write hers too, maybe embellish it and mix it with my own. It was sad, all of it, dismal really. It could be a best seller!

Grandmother continued on, "After World War II ended, money was tight. Noreen was the only one working. She was a librarian working at the main branch of the *New York Public Library*. She would spend her free time in the Village downtown where she told me she had a boyfriend stashed away from the prying eyes of her much older sister, Eileen."

The phone rang interrupting the story. "Sorry, it's probably one of those dinner time callers asking for money; be right back."

A half an hour later, Grandmother came back. I guessed it wasn't a telemarketer but she wasn't offering up any info. She went right back to the story.

"The other sister, Anna, used to meet me after school. It all started when I was about fifteen. I was small for my age and a good generator of sympathy from the local pawn guy. Anna was a tricky one. She would make purchases on credit in the morning and return them to the same store in the afternoon. They would give her cash back even though she bought on credit. She would also pawn everything that wasn't nailed down to buy alcohol," Grandmother said, shaking her head "poor Anna, she wanted to be a wife and a mother more than anything else. But she fell in unlucky love with a married man named Johnny, who wouldn't leave his wife. Every afternoon, Aunt Eileen volunteered to make dinner for the priests at the rectory; she'd be gone for hours. Anna and Johnny would drink. Johnny showed me how to mix drinks but most of the time, they both just passed the bottles around. Anna would pass out and I would be left alone with Johnny. He never called me by my name; he called me, *the stray.*"

Grandmother sighed before continuing, "most evenings when Aunt Eileen returned home, she was too tired to notice I had slurred and sleepy speech. She didn't notice until Anna lost her mind and had to go one way to what they called a *rest home* and I had to go to another," Grandmother stopped short before she spoke again, this time speaking quietly like she was talking to herself, "he would be about sixty something now, the baby I had, Johnny's baby."

I quickly turned from the stove to look over at Grandmother but she again had that faraway glaze in her eyes.

"I only saw him for a few minutes before they took him away. I had been there for six months and three days waiting around with others like me, waiting for our babies to be born and snatched away to the *better life,* they promised. All of us, in our shared earthly Purgatory, kept our heads down, our eyes staring over our growing bellies as if in a symmetrical state of apprehension while avoiding, but always feeling the judgmental eyes of the nuns in charge upon us."

Grandmother was not talking to me now, she was venting, expelling it, probably for the first time. Tears were swimming around in my eyes; I loved her already. It was sad hearing this story of her hard life, then suddenly she changed the subject.

"Your mother called today, while you were out. She had some news."

"Oh, yeah, what is it? Is she joining a cult or something?"

"There's a warrant out for your father. Apparently, he's been doing some illicit business with pictures on the Internet. Meghan wasn't forthcoming with details. Do you know anything about this? You seem to be afraid of him. Did he do something to you?"

The confession about the baby and the quick question to me about my father seemed to linger together mid-air over the stove, mixing and melting into one another. I turned back, held on tight to the sides of the stove and leaned my face into the steam rising from the caramelizing carrots to hide my shame.

"Not just me," I said without meaning to. I didn't want to tell her; I didn't want to tell anyone, but he was here hanging around, hunting me down. He and his entourage were stalking me, loitering around on the street, waiting to pounce.

Grandmother's hand reached in front of me, shielding me with her arm like the wing of a mother bird cradling her nest. She escorted me to the dining room and sat me down at the table. I was helpless; my body felt limp, empty of all substance. She kept the kitchen door open while she finished cooking the dinner I'd started. The carrots were in a sad, soggy state, but she placed them on a plate full of salad greens and sautéed the marinated chicken before adding it to the plate. It had all been revived. Grandmother sat next to me at the table, instead of at the head where she usually sat. It was if her formal self was shedding its skin and she was relaxing into a new role as caretaker. She ate fast and didn't ask me anything else about my father.

"When I returned to Aunt Eileen's almost seven months later, she was changed. In those days, it was always the girl's fault. The thinking was you must have done something to attract the unwanted affection. It was hard to live there after that. She rarely spoke more than was necessary. I learned to make myself scarce when I heard her mattress creak in the morning. I wondered if she regretted taking me in or was feeling overwhelmed with guilt for having put me in harm's way. Maybe this is how your mother is feeling now. Some people cope by distancing themselves; they can't bear the recognition of the source of their guilt."

I was pretty positive this was not the case with Meghan but I kept quiet.

"I watched Aunt Eileen more than I spoke to her. She was a heavy-set woman who wore navy blue like it was a religious habit; she never wore pants. When she went out, it was always in a dress with a full skirt which had faded polka dots over the entire fabric. She wore a small hat too, but I can't remember her shoes no matter how hard I try. It's funny the things that stick in your mind. I wonder what you'll remember about me. She never wore make-up, she just dusted her natural ruddy complexion with a powder that came in a round box with a big puff inside. *Coty* made it and it went all over the place. She used *Sweetheart Soap*; it was lead heavy and you couldn't kill it. It lasted for months which is probably why they don't make it anymore," she laughed, "every morning Aunt Eileen would put on a house dress, it was flowered and multi-colored. She dust-mopped the entire apartment and I would lift my legs to accommodate her mopping but nothing was ever said. She did always give me a parting look, every afternoon, before she'd make her way out the door to the rectory."

"How could you stay there? It must have su…been awful," I asked, although I knew the answer. She was a kid, where could she go? I wanted her to keep talking forever so she wouldn't ask me anymore questions. I barely listened. I was lucky I had her. I had someplace to go; I got out.

"Oh, I was sad most of the time and ashamed but I couldn't just hang around doing nothing. This was frowned upon and looking back, I suppose, they thought I'd find my way into trouble again. Noreen got me a job at the library; I worked there after school and then full-time after I graduated. I stacked books and returned the ones the patrons left behind on tables. That's where I met your grandfather. One day, a gentleman came in, approached me, shyly at first. He showed me a book which was five years overdue. He looked me straight in the eye with his own pleading deep blue ones that drew me right in. It was some show; I was hooked. *I'm a good actress,* I told him. I came up with a scenario and told the staff I found the book misplaced on the wrong shelf all these years. I was the heroine of the 42nd Street branch. It was a win-win situation all around. But after a few weeks, he started coming in every day. It turned out there were four more books and each one was five years overdue. The fine was a hefty one-hundred-thirty-seven dollars. It was more than I earned in a week, but he nonchalantly handed it all over. He came in almost every day for a whole month. He would leave one yellow rose on top of the books waiting on the table to be stacked where he knew I would find it. The yellow roses soon turned to red ones and we were married there years later."

My emotions got the better of me, exhaustion had set in and I had fallen asleep and I missed the romance part of the story. I missed hearing about her dates with Grandfather and the details of their wedding. I knew she'd tell me another time. I was barely awake. I was sliding down in the chair.

"Jenna, don't slouch. Go to bed if you're tired." She spoke in an uncharacteristically loud voice snapping me back to reality. I was tired but doubted I'd sleep tonight after hearing all about Grandmother's life. But I was wrong, I fell asleep again and slept through until morning.

Chapter Seven

The sun wasn't entirely up, it was barely 5 am, when I decided to see the New York City morning. I took the back door out of the kitchen and ran down the stairs to take the elevator on the next floor. I was still in runaway mode all these weeks later and waited on edge for something to happen. My grandmother kept trying to mine me for information, told me her stuff, hoping I'd say something like, *oh, yeah, you think that was bad, listen to this.*

When I reached the lobby, the night doorman was standing on the sidewalk smoking a cigarette. I went in the opposite direction and around the corner toward the park. The air was crisp, warm but not hot and it smelled clean. It seemed like the whole city had gone through a rinse cycle overnight. The rhythmic music of traffic and people rushing about normally in sync was muted in the early morning. It was a nice change from the five o'clock rush Gypsy and I were stuck in after our adventure in Riverside Park. The whole place was like an orchestra if you stopped to listen. Sights and sounds were conducted in some kind of harmonious tempo. The sudden interruption of an ambulance or police siren did not disrupt it and only seemed to add to the flavor. It was like a conductor was turning his baton toward a new section of the New York City street orchestra.

The park was mostly empty with a few straggling joggers and homeless people sacked out on several benches. It was too ominous looking so I turned back toward home. The doorman was on the curb now, hailing a cab. I turned to look at him and felt something grab my arm.

"Hello, Jenna," my father said through his teeth. "You aren't eighteen yet, Missy, you still belong to me." A few more feet and I could have been inside instead of out here on the sidewalk.

Missy, huh? A spontaneous giggle burped up out of nowhere. The flight attendant I met on the second leg of my escape was what I was thinking about for some reason.

He shook me hard. "You think this is funny? What have you been telling your grandmother? There were cops at my apartment. I'm an artist, my pictures are art, nothing more."

"I didn't say anything to anybody." I turned and tried to pull away from him. Out of the corner of my eye, I saw the same blonde woman leaning on a dark blue Toyota Camry. It was parked a few feet away on 79th Street. The windows were tinted but I could see a small figure in the back. Panic set in as my father pulled me toward it. I knew my feet were on the ground but I couldn't feel them. I felt faint but pulled myself together and yelled, "Get your hands off of me!"

The doorman was taking a tip from a resident who was getting into a taxi. He closed the door to the cab and turned to me. "Miss O'Connor are you okay? Is this man bothering you?"

My father let go of me, moved toward the Camry, looked back once and said, "You won't get away with this, Jenna."

The doorman guided me toward a chair and brought me a bottle of water. "Should I call your grandmother?"

"No, I'm okay now, thanks." I suppose the time had come to tell her. I'd never be free if I didn't.

The doorman, Nick, according to the pin on his jacket, insisted on taking me upstairs himself. Grandmother was in the kitchen with Katrina preparing for the day's cooking lessons. She'd been neglecting her students ever since I had arrived. Nick held me by the arm and handed me off to Grandmother. I didn't feel real; I didn't feel anything at all. My whole life was like a movie being played out without my control and this was just another scene.

"What happened?" Grandmother extended her arms to pull me in after wiping her hands on the towel tucked into her apron.

"He's out there. He's trying to take me back."

"Who's out there? What are you talking about, Jenna?"

"My father, Alan, he's here, stalking me."

"Now, are you ready to tell what this is all about? Your father is wanted in California. We have to report this. If you don't want to talk to me, it's okay, but it will help you to share it, talk to someone. There's a therapist right here in the building who helped me after your grandfather died. Maybe she can help you deal with your feelings."

I felt numb. I was not even a person, I never was. I was a thing, an object; how could I feel anything? The only thing I felt right now was my head nodding in agreement to whatever it was she was suggesting. Grandmother picked up the phone, just as the doorbell rang.

"Hey, what're you doing? You want to hang out?" Gypsy was breathless from running up several flights.

"Can I go down to Gypsy's?" I yelled to Grandmother.

"Hello, Gabrielle," Grandmother yelled back. I opened my eyes wide and stared at Gypsy.

"Oh, sometimes I have dinner here when Adele's going to be gone for a while." Jealously roared up inside of me; I was the stranger here, the newbie in the already established hive. I was the outsider; Gypsy and my grandmother were a "we," already a unit. Gypsy had been spending time with my grandmother while I didn't even know either of them existed. This was Meghan's fault, all of it. I had so many other things to worry about, but this hurt and there was no one here to take the blame. Not yet, anyway.

Meghan was coming here, probably already on her way. Home was closing in on me, coming to get me and take me back. I hadn't seen my mother in weeks; she never even asked to speak to me when she called. This wasn't a reunion I was looking forward to. Maybe she'd put me in that fantasy home for troubled girls. Here was the panic, again. I guess I could feel something. The walls were closing in and I needed to be somewhere else. Meeting Gypsy's mother was as good an excuse as any to escape.

When we walked in, Adele was on the phone. She nodded hello in my direction and motioned with one hand for us to leave the room. She was a big woman dressed in a caftan with a scarf covering her head. Gypsy waved her hand for me to follow her into her room. She put in a DVD and we settled on the bed to watch. I couldn't say what we saw; I was numb from my father's assault. It all seemed surreal. Ignoring him and pretending that part of my life was over wasn't an option. I could see that now.

When the movie ended, I noticed it wasn't even the same one we had started watching. I missed two movies while wondering what was going to happen next. Gypsy stood up and stretched her long arms up over her head. "What do you want to do now? Are you on Facebook? We can look people up; do you have an old boyfriend we can check on? It'll be fun."

"I have to go home," I said it, the word home, even though I wasn't sure where home was. I have to see a therapist friend of my grandmother's." I didn't know why I shared this. She had a magnetic way of sucking information out of me. I was not going to tell her about Jude, no matter what. Last thing I needed now was to find out he was in prison because of me. Gypsy interrupted my self-generating drama. "Oh, Dr. G, she's cool."

"Do you just know everyone on the planet?" Gypsy shrugged. "It's a small building."

I left her room and made my way down the hall and through the kitchen to the front door. Adele was still on the phone when I closed the door behind me. It was after three.

Chapter Eight

The student cooks were gone for the day but the whole apartment was filled with a medley of aromas. Grandmother was drinking tea in the kitchen. Tea, the elixir for all that ailed you. My mother drank it like it was part of a religious ritual. Judging by the used, dried out tea bags and the diluted pale liquid, Grandmother was several cups down. She looked up when I came in.

"Let's talk now."

"Okay, what do you want to talk about? You have more stories to tell me?" I knew I was being obnoxious. I knew exactly what she wanted to talk about. I didn't know where to start or how.

"I think your mother will want to take you back to California with her. If this isn't what you want, tell me now and I'll do everything I can to stop it from happening."

"I don't want to go back there, ever."

Grandmother put her arm around me in the same mother bird fashion and picked up the phone with her other hand, *O'Connor, Stanton and Smith,* a disembodied voice announced from the other end adding, *Law Offices.* It was the office of my grandfather's old firm.

"Mr. Stanton, please, this is Katherine O'Connor speaking; it's rather urgent." Grandmother spoke in a confident, authoritative tone. She gave Mr. Stanton a brief synopsis of what she thought was going on with my father. "There's a warrant out for him in California; I'm not sure for what, but there are hints of online pornographic activities involving children or worse. His name is Alan Rose, I think he goes by A.J. Rose. Do an investigation and get back to me as soon as possible. I also need to know if I have a legal standing here in

New York with regards to custody of my seventeen-year old granddaughter, Jenna, same last name, Rose. She'll be in harm's way if she is returned to her parents. She came on her own to New York, to me." She hung up looking relieved. If I had to guess, I'd say, she was still the queen of the law firm.

"I'm messed up, Grandmother."

"In what way?" I just shook my head, eyes down.

How could I possibly tell her I'd been like a prisoner in the lake house for most of my life; that my father used me as his model, taking naked pictures of me for as long as I could remember, and that I still had no idea why or what he did it for, although I have an idea now, an idea I didn't want to think about.

"It'll be okay now, you have help. You found your way to me, this is your refuge in the storm. Try to remember it isn't where you start out in life that matters, but where you end up. Keep that in your head like a mantra. It's how I got through all those rough times. Nothing lasts forever."

I swear, I was about to blurt out the whole sordid story, at least the parts I remembered but the doorbell rang. It was the doctor.

"Hello, Christine, this is my granddaughter, Jenna. Jenna, this is Dr. Christine Gautier."

"Hello," I said quietly, feeling the hot rush of shame surge through me like a current of electricity. Dr. Gautier looked more like a gypsy, like she could tell my fortune without much trouble. Her hair was long and wispy; it fell down her back like silk on an ear of corn. She took my hand firmly in her own and looked me right in the eye.

"Is everything okay? When you didn't come down for your session, I decided to come up here." She spoke with a slight French accent, "Do you want to talk or should we do this another time?"

"It's up to Jenna, Christine. Personally, I think she needs some support right now, but it's up to her." I nodded without realizing it and Grandmother left the room.

"Jenna, I want you to know even though your grandmother and I are friends, everything that you say to me stays between us. Our sessions will be a private matter. No one will know unless you give me permission to tell or you tell someone on your own. Do you understand?"

"Yes, I guess so." I excused myself and went to the bathroom. I washed my face, glancing at myself in the mirror. My hair looked damp, my face was red and I felt feverish. I sat on the edge of the tub, put my head down between my knees and took a deep breath. I took another. *What's going to happen to me?* I asked my mirror self. What if something happened to my grandmother? Meghan didn't want me. What kind of parents were they anyway? *Maybe I'd been kidnapped?* I thought, hoping this was the truth. It would explain why they never seemed to care and why Grandmother never had a chance to meet me before now. I suddenly became furious. Anger, I decided, was better than fear. Fear would keep me down; anger, I hoped would keep me focused and help me to keep going.

Dr. Gautier waited patiently. She asked me basic questions: "How old are you? Where did you go to school? Do you have a lot of friends?" At least now, I could say I had a friend, a real friend. A few weeks ago, I'd have been lying if I said I had friends. I still wasn't sure about Jude. I didn't even know his last name. I didn't want to talk about any of this. I felt like a freak. For a minute, I considered bolting again. I still had Meghan's Amex card.

"Why did you come to New York on your own? That was very brave."

"I was alone, I had to." I stopped mid-sentence.

"Okay, Jenna, tell me about your mother." I told her about Meghan's business and how she was rarely home, and how I was always with my father until he left.

"Tell me about your father; were you close to him?" Close, was she serious? I started to cry, I never cried. I didn't think I could, I never did, ever. I reached up and touched the alien tears with my fingertips.

"Do you want to tell me now? What is the truth, Jenna?"

Being in a position where you had nothing to lose wasn't a good feeling. Everything was stacked against me. My mother was on her way here; she would take me back to California and leave me as bait for my father. He didn't want me for his *art* anymore, but he didn't want me running around on my own, spilling out bits of the truth everywhere I went. There was no reason I could think of not to trust this woman. Grandmother obviously had no loyalty to either one of my parents. I blurted it out in one breath.

"My father took pictures of me naked and stuff since I was very small until I turned thirteen." I knew it wasn't the whole truth but it was a start and it was out there now, drifting in the air.

"Your father's in trouble. He sold pictures of children on the Internet. Did you know this?" I shook my head, but I guessed a part of me knew. Why else would he have done this?

"While there's no blatant sexual abuse in the ones found so far, there is what is called, *Intent to do harm.* It's probable there are pictures of you, as well, in with those which were confiscated. You will need to be brave now so he can be stopped. This is very harmful, not only to you but to the others as well. It's going to be essential you tell me as much as you can remember. Tell me first, so you can be comfortable speaking with law enforcement."

"You mean the police?"

"Yes, Jenna, and possibly testify in court down the road. We are getting ahead of ourselves but you must be prepared. Do you want to remain here with your grandmother? Now is the time to say so. Your mother's rights of custody will be questioned if she knowingly left you in harm's way. Do you think she knew what your father was doing?"

"I don't know," I told her, but Meghan had to have known something. "Truthfully, I don't think she cared." It was a bold thing to say but my mother didn't seem to care about me so why should I care what happened to her.

"Jenna, I need to ask you one more thing and I want you to think carefully before answering. It may upset you but it's important. Did your father ever mention, *Teasing Tots*? It's a website."

"No, did he sell pictures of me, put them on that site? Do you know, tell me please?"

"It's okay, Jenna, I don't know if this is true. It's possible he did, but I don't know for sure. I need to tell you something else." Oh, God, now what? She seemed to have more to tell me than I had to tell her.

"Did you know your grandmother's a wealthy woman?" I'd have to be blind and comatose not to have realized this, but I said nothing. "Having money can make you powerful; she may not seem it but she's very strong and has endured a lot in this life. She can handle this and she can and will give you a good life from now on. You have to trust her. We can talk to her together, if you'd like, we can do it right now."

I had the same unreal feeling zap right through to my bones; my face felt hot. I felt like people were pointing at me saying, *Look, there she is!* I told this to Dr. G; she nodded and said, "I understand, but there's no reason for you to feel this way. You did nothing wrong."

Dr. Gautier was a person who made you feel like you'd finally found your place. It happened in an instant, this feeling she really cared, like some mothers I'd read about. Or maybe it was just her exotic French accent. But still my hands were trembling when I opened the door to call to Grandmother. She came in, sat down and we switched roles. Now, it was my turn to tell her my story.

A part of me wanted to tell it all right then, let it out. I had nothing to lose. Some things I couldn't say and I didn't remember all of it. I vaguely remembered there being other people in the room at times. It was one of those blurry memories where you weren't entirely certain it happened at all, like an abstract dream.

"I don't think my mother ever wanted me." I hesitated to look over at Grandmother. Even though, it was her daughter I was talking about, she seemed detached.

"Go on, Jenna." My mouth was dry; I was sweating but felt cold. I took a sip of water and continued. "She was hardly ever home. She left me with my father all the time. It was nearly always just the two of us. Meghan's business was her real family. But my father used me for his. He took pictures of me. I guess you could call me his model. I didn't want to do it but I had to. I never saw any of those pictures. Then it was all over."

I didn't share everything, I couldn't. He had taken some horrible pictures of me; pried into my inner being until I had no self. How could I make them understand? I lost, but how could you lose what you'd never had? I only knew what I lost because I read so much about how other people lived.

"Will I have to testify in court if my father goes to jail?"

"Jenna, it will take months before that happens if it happens at all. As hard as this is, I suggest you try not to focus on it. Try to concentrate on your new life here. I'll prepare you when the time comes and be there with you in court if necessary. I suggest we meet every week this summer and then we can see how you are adjusting. Does that sound okay with you?"

"Yes, I guess." But how should I know if that would help? I never had anyone to talk to before, except for Jude and that was for a brief moment in time. I wished I'd come here years ago. Maybe I was too far gone now. Living in the aftermath of that life was all I wanted now. I didn't want to be a victim who needed curing; I didn't want revenge, all I needed was to forget. I wanted to scream: *Get it off of me.*

Dr. G gave me a hug and chatted quietly with Grandmother about some building gossip, before leaving the apartment.

Chapter Nine

Showering for a good hour or so was as therapeutic as talking. I tried desperately to scrub the jinx off my skin. Jinxed was what I decided I was. Really, I came all this way, escaped from people who didn't care enough to be with me when I was right there with them and now they were racing across the country to get me back, suddenly faithful and devoted parents. It was all for show.

Grandmother was standing in the kitchen facing the sink. I had my head down in a towel, drying my hair. I heard Meghan before I saw her; she was sobbing softly at the kitchen table. Grandmother was ignoring her. They seemed to be doing an apathy dance around each other. Between sobs, Meghan took dainty sips of tea from Grandmother's best china. She had a way of making tragedy seem elegant, like she was auditioning for a part. She got up from her chair when she saw me. Grandmother wiped her hands on her apron and readied herself to rescue me. Meghan came toward me with outstretched arms, wrapped them around me in a faux sign of affection. I stood still with my arms rigid at my side while she whispered in my ear, "It's going to be all right." Suddenly raising her voice, she stepped back. "Now, Jenna, everything is going to be all right, I put the house up for sale. We'll move where no one will know us. I'll sell my business. I mean, after all, how is this going to look to everyone who knows me? We can change our names and…"

Just like that, she thought everything was going to be okay, wiped away with a big eraser. *No*, I'd *found a home and it wasn't with her, it never was.* Grandmother was about to say something but I raised my hand and gently placed it against her chest shaking my head, no. She stepped back. I felt empowered for once by this new-found support system and I told my mother clearly in a strong voice, "I'm not coming back to California with you."

"Listen, Jenna, don't start with me. I was sick with worry. I came here to get you and now you have to help me through this. How will it look if you're not with me? What will people think? They'll think I had something to do with all this, that's what they'll think. They'll…"

I didn't let her finish. "Listen to me now, Meghan, this isn't about you." She came close with her hand raised to slap me. Grandmother reached her first, grabbed her hand derailing the slap. She held Meghan's hand and stared hard before she said, "Could you be any more selfish? I think it's best if you go to a hotel or back to California. It's obvious you aren't going to be of any help here."

"Stay out of this, Mother. You always did put yourself in the middle of things. Keep in mind, Jenna is still underage and in my custody."

"I wouldn't be making any idle threats if I were you, Meghan. You neglected Jenna and you know it; you put her in the path of that husband of yours. I think you'd better leave Jenna be. Let me help her."

Grandmother finally came up for air, confident she'd get her way. She grabbed my hand, led me out of the kitchen while leaving Meghan behind in shock, with nothing but her thoughts to keep her company.

When the door slammed, I started to cry. Twice in one day, tears that had been bottled up for a lifetime came gushing out of me. Grandmother took me in her arms. My pulse was pounding, racing from my chest up to my neck. I tried breathing through my mouth.

"You are safe, calm down, Jenna."

"Not with my father still out there." I looked over at the photograph of my mother; glazed and frozen, a snapshot in a time I knew nothing about. She sat smugly looking out at a future she thought inevitable; her legacy of wealth and power, a legacy she kept all to herself. It was all there in her photo eyes as it was now in the flesh, the demeanor of denial and remorselessness. She was a mean girl then, I could see it, the callous shell forming slowly and taking root. Why hadn't she just aborted me? Instead she let him erase me with an inch-by-inch termination, retroactively fulfilling the wish I knew she'd made long ago in the photograph on the mantle.

"Jenna… are you okay? What are you thinking about? Here's some tea."

Ugh, I hated tea, it reminded me of the flu. But I drank it anyway. It tasted like dishwater. She meant well. "Thanks, Grandmother."

"None of this is your fault, you know that, don't you? If anything, it's our fault, your grandfather and mine. We spoiled your mother. She never could put anyone else first. We were too soft with her. Your grandfather adored her and she knew it. He couldn't stand to be away from her for a minute. She used this to her advantage. She had learned from the master, her paternal grandmother who was a controlling and practiced manipulator. I was very different from anyone she'd ever known in her elite circle. She tried to make me over into someone resembling a younger version of herself. I resisted, so she moved on to weave Meghan in her image. We relocated to California to have our own life and Grandfather opened a law office there. Once she was old enough, Meghan went to New York every summer to be with her grandmother. It was a mistake, but your grandfather wouldn't listen to me. So, Meghan was molded into a self-absorbed indulged kid.

After my mother-in-law died, we moved back to New York. Her real estate holdings were vast and too difficult to manage from across the country. Grandfather was her only child. I don't think Meghan ever got over the loss. She was a teenager by then and didn't want to move. She blamed us, of course. She went back to California for college and never returned. Your grandfather was devastated. He kept his San Francisco office open in case Meghan decided to pursue law but she had no interest. She became someone I never wanted her to be, she became her grandmother."

"Why did she even have me?"

"We didn't know where she was after she graduated from college. She had inherited money and didn't need our support. We didn't know she was pregnant. We finally hired a detective and he found her, but she refused to let us have any contact with her or access to you. We didn't know if she was married. It was a tremendous loss not to be there for the birth of our first grandchild. It's something I will never get back and certainly didn't deserve, to be deprived of my only grandchild. Your grandfather never got over the loss; it changed him. He became sullen and withdrawn. I suspect that he subconsciously blamed me for all of it. It's always the woman's fault. But Meghan was wrong and karma may be coming home to roost now." Grandmother smiled through tear-soaked eyes.

"But you're here now and that's what's most important. We'll get through this together, you and I."

I wasn't used to people telling it like it is. Grandmother was so different from my mother it was hard to believe they were even related. I didn't know what to say; I didn't blame her. Plenty of people were spoiled, I bet, plenty of people were indulged too and they didn't throw their daughters into a wolf's den. I changed the subject.

"Do you really think that I'll have to go to court to testify against my father if they catch him?" Then, I added, "Do you really believe in karma?"

I knew how it worked, not karma but the court system. I was their best witness. I knew he was still out there waiting. He had to know I held the key to his downfall. I wondered to myself, *what Emily Dickinson would have done if this happened to her. Most likely, she would write volumes of cryptic poetry. Who could she have told? Who would have believed a recluse in white living in a time when women were the property of first their fathers and then their husbands?* I guess I was lucky I had choices. I didn't have any talent for writing though. In those days I'd have been out of luck.

I was off in a fantasy world and didn't even remember asking questions when all of a sudden, Grandmother said, "Oh, they'll catch him; they always do. It's just a matter of time but try not to worry about that now. Get yourself adjusted to living here with me. Do you think you can do that? Oh, and yes, I believe in karma. A. J. Rose will get what's coming to him."

Grandmother spoke with the confidence of someone who'd been used to getting her own way. She didn't say, *I'll try to get custody*, she said, *I'm going to get at least temporary custody of you.* Sighing hard helped me to relax but the truth was I was afraid of my parents. The fear lingered and I didn't know how to be unafraid.

Well, Grandmother was right about my father, they found him, he was arrested and was headed back to California in police custody. I wondered what happened to the woman and the girl who were with him. I wanted to concentrate on other things but the shadow of Alan lingered and remnants of those memories came around every night when my head hit the pillow. Pushing them aside at night was tough but during the day, Gypsy made it easy to forget.

Chapter Ten

August was a strange month. The heat made us lazy, then the air became cooler and it reminded me of California. I had pangs of homesickness, I couldn't imagine why. It was too much newness. I was going into my last year of high school and I'd finally be going back to a real school. Meghan had agreed to let me stay here. Things were starting to look up, for now at least.

Gypsy talked Grandmother into enrolling me in the same private all-girls school she attended. I knew Gypsy hated it there but she said having me there would make it better for her. It was the first selfish thing she'd done so far.

It was mid-August, I was scheduled for an interview and a placement test. I could tell the school administrators were unsure of me, a home-schooled kid who may have emotional baggage. I felt like I was wearing it all, and I still felt the pointing people who weren't really there, saying, *Look! There she is.*

The headmistress asked me questions, "Who is your favorite author or poet?" I could talk for hours about books. When I told her Nabokov and Emily Dickinson, she seemed stunned. I knew she didn't believe me so I recited a few lines from a Dickinson poem, a random one so she didn't think I'd rehearsed. The placement test was a different story. The math part set off my panic mode. What if they didn't take me?

I saw Gypsy smoking near the curb outside when I finished and left the building. "I think I blew the math part, what if they don't take me? Where will I go then?"

"Don't worry, they'll take you."

"I don't know, Gypsy, it was pretty hard."

"They'll take you, trust me."

"How are you so sure of everything all the time?"

"Because I know how it works."

"Yeah, okay, so how does it work?'

"Your grandmother will write them a check, that's how it works."

I had no answer because I didn't believe it. I just had to wait and see. The rest of the summer was spent lazing around. It was barely 9 a.m. one morning, when I heard Gypsy's voice.

"Hey, guess what? Wilhelmina called, I have a go-see. Want to come with me?"

Ever since I heard Gypsy was a model, I wondered about it; what the real world of modeling was like. I assumed it was glamorous, not like the sneaky behind closed door-photography Alan was into. I'd never heard the name Wilhelmina before; I was dying to get a look at her. I imagined a flabby, sloppy woman whose flesh spilled out over her chair and dragged on the floor. I pictured a woman who looked kind of like the character, *Margery, the trash heap,* from the old *Fraggle Rock* reruns. I couldn't imagine her looking any different with that name. But as it turned out, there was no Wilhelmina, it was just the name of the agency. Gypsy was picked to be a runway model for fashion week. No one even glanced in my direction; I was as short as Gypsy was tall. It was just as well, I didn't want to pose for anyone ever again.

Gypsy and I were inseparable ever since the first day in the elevator, but now we'd had too much summer. There was a week left before school started. I got in and had to start earlier because I was new. I pretended it was a fluke. I was afraid to ask Grandmother if she'd bribed anyone with a donation. I didn't want to know.

Chapter Eleven

It rained for three straight days before finally stopping and breaking the August humidity. We were bored with television and everything else, "I know, let's go to visit my grandmother," Gypsy suggested while jumping up off of the reclining chair where she'd taken up semi-permanent residence.

"I thought she was dead; didn't you tell me she died?"

"Yeah, she did, but I found her and we can still visit; c'mon let's go."

"I don't know about this, Gypsy, I think it's weird."

"Okay, so if your grandmother dies, you won't go and visit her grave?" She stood over me with her hands on her hips, put her head to one side and pursed her lips.

"Okay, you have a valid point."

The three days of rain cooled the air somewhat. My California-raised body had no tolerance for the intense heat but today was bearable. Gypsy stopped at her apartment for supplies. I was not sure what supplies she needed to visit her dead grandmother and I didn't want to ask.

We walked up Broadway to the 96th Street station to get the number two-subway train to the Bronx. I should've asked where Gypsy's grandmother was buried. I stupidly assumed she was somewhere in Manhattan. Gypsy was fearless; I was not. I didn't think I could handle a mugging or anything else after my ordeal with my father. It was too late now. I felt myself chill as the train pulled into the station. It was my third time on the subway.

It was Saturday, the car was filled with shoppers guarding their purchases with knees locked around shopping bags. No one was smiling or engaging in conversation, but everyone groaned as if on cue, when the Mariachi band appeared dressed in native clothing. They weren't bad as musicians, if you liked that sort of thing, but they were unwanted intruders invading everyone's personal space. They reminded me of my father; it made them the anti-entertainers. I was lost in that thought when Gypsy poked me with her elbow gesturing for me to get up. We were there already, in the Bronx on East 233rd Street. It was a three-block walk from the station to the gates of *Woodlawn Cemetery.*

Chapter Twelve

I prepared myself to be creeped out as we approached the gate on Webster Avenue, but I let out a gasp when we passed between the carved facades which stood imposingly on either side of the opening to the cemetery. To me, they seemed like big stone welcome mats.

"Gypsy, what is this place? It's like a royal estate not a cemetery; not like I've ever seen." I'd only seen pictures, of course. I'd never been to a cemetery before.

"Geez, close your mouth, Jenna, you haven't seen it yet."

"What, seen what?"

We walked through the winding tree-lined road where sculptured angels seemed to be pointing the way. I felt like I'd arrived at the city of the dead. It was comforting and peaceful, not scary at all. I glanced over at a large stone structure which seemed too modern for this place. It was a black, shiny stone billboard-like tribute to the memory of the jazz musician, Miles Davis.

"Wow," I said too loud. "I could stay here."

"Don't be stupid, that's ridiculous." Gypsy shook her head and gave me one of her looks. She was intent on finding her grandmother. She'd been here before but she seemed to have forgotten the way. She was always so self-assured, no matter what and she would never, ever ask for directions. It took an hour to find the grave. Her grandmother's headstone was less ornate than most of the others. It had a serene appearance with softer, young looking cherub angels hanging off the top. Her name, *Ella F. Booker,* was boldly carved in dark lettering.

Gypsy plopped herself down on the edge of the headstone and pulled out a sandwich from her bag. She handed me half; I wasn't hungry and waved her off. I reached for the cell phone

Grandmother had bought me and started to call her. She wasn't home when I left and I had forgotten to leave a note.

"Put that away, it's disrespectful."

"You're eating a sandwich."

"Eating is a natural thing, cellphones aren't. Besides, they weren't even invented when my grandmother was alive, she won't know what it is."

"Seriously, you think I'll scare her to death or something?" I immediately regretted the comment. Gypsy locked her eyes with mine. I looked down and then up again at her.

"I'm sorry, that was rude."

She frowned briefly and then seemed to forget the whole thing. She introduced me to her grandmother as the *best friend I ever had.* The whole scene reminded me of my grandmother's story about visiting Jimmy after he died and having to give him all the news of life going on without him.

"Thanks, Gypsy, you're the only friend I've ever had." I wasn't ready to tell her about Jude. "So, what's the *F* stand for?"

"Dunno," she said with her mouth full of slimy tuna. "I won't dare ask Adele, she won't tell me anyway."

There were loads of celebrities in this place, Miles Davis, Herman Melville. It was like Eden. I wondered if Gypsy's grandmother was famous for something. It seemed someone must have loved her. Her gravesite was taken care of.

"Somebody must take care of this grave; there are flowering plants here. It was so hot all summer, someone must water them.

"This is a famous cemetery, a landmark. Strangers take care of it. You don't think my mother does it do you? Please, you met her, sort of. She wouldn't even get off of the phone to meet my best friend."

I didn't think Gypsy noticed her mother wasn't interested in meeting me. But, I'd asked enough questions. I stood up and brushed the loose grass from my shorts. We wandered around, it was peaceful. The dead must like it here; it was better than out here on earth with the people who still had pulses.

"This place is awesome."

"What's wrong with you? This is a cemetery, duh! You can't get in unless you're dead!" Gypsy rolled her eyes and we walked further onto the grounds checking out the headstones and mausoleums. Gypsy was not really interested, but I was fascinated. She grew up in New York in a world of celebrity. Adele worked with them and when Gypsy was little, she would take her to parties and present her like a trophy, until she got fresh. That ended that. But some of them remembered her and called her sometimes. I thought it was cool.

"Wow, look it's Herman Melville." Later I spotted Duke Ellington and James Cash Penney.

"Who?" Gypsy rolled her eyes again. "It's not like they're going to jump up and give you and autograph. Who is he, anyway?"

"J.C. Penney," I said and then I kept quiet for the rest of the trip home.

This time, the subway train creeped along back to Manhattan. There were no entertainers on board, there were just ordinary people returning to ordinary lives who sat side by side for the first and last time. I wished for a minute I could attach myself to one of them and avoid the impending doom I was always sensing on my horizon. Instead, I chose to think of something else, "Want to sleep over tonight? Isn't Adele leaving?"

Chapter Thirteen

The irresistible lure of something baking thrusted us toward Grandmother's kitchen. But there were boxes filling the entryway sideswiping us on our way. They were all from Amazon and they were all addressed to me. It was like television Christmas. Gypsy scrutinized the boxes, "Don't get too excited, it's just school stuff." Even this was exciting for me. I unpacked the first box and out came my uniform.

"Go try it on," Grandmother said while coming from the kitchen to see what we were doing. Her hands were stained red. A berry pie of some sort would be on the dessert menu tonight.

When I came out wearing a sea of plaid, every one burst out laughing including Katrina. "Lord, have mercy," she said before returning to the kitchen. Her hands were also stained red.

The uniform consisted of a skirt and a stiff white cotton blouse which, according to Gypsy had to be kept tucked in at all times. It looked like the outfit my grandmother was wearing on the day I arrived. It clung annoyingly to the middle of my knee.

"Do you think there's time to shorten it before school starts?" I didn't want to draw negative attention to myself. I'd watched enough high school drama on T.V. to know what went on.

"Forget it, that's the length it has to be. Just roll it up like the rest of us when no one is looking." Gypsy was off in the corner, leafing through a magazine, making off the cuff comments.

"There's a warm weather version which is this one. You can wear this until October and then the winter regulation uniform is enforced. Don't get your hopes up, they're all bad."

"Wow, what a frumpy thing, even I wouldn't wear it. It reminds me of my own Catholic school uniform. They haven't progressed much."

"The headmistress probably taught you, Mrs. O."

After I put the uniform boxes in my room, Gypsy and I went to the kitchen to see what was cooking. Chopped sugared strawberries were bubbling in a pot on the stove. Katrina added a spoonful of cornstarch to thicken it. She stirred the molten mass and then shut off the flame to let the whole thing cool before putting it into the already baked pie shell. The lingering aroma was enough to keep us homebound for the night.

Chapter Fourteen

School started two days after Labor Day; I had chills and permanent nausea. My classmates were blonde, all of them. They were blonde whether they were born blonde or not. I was not going to fit in. I knew right away why Gypsy hated it here. It was cliché. I was in another episode of the movie version of my life. I didn't have time for mean girl cliquey stuff. I needed to make up for lost time. I had to take SATs in a few weeks, then college applications would be due and I was behind and panicked.

I wondered if my mother had planned for me to attend college at all or if she would have ever let me leave the lake house. I had not heard from her since she returned to California. I didn't know her new address and neither did Grandmother.

I was the only new kid in the senior class; of course, I was. Why would anyone start a new school in their last year? The whole class was like a well-oiled machine. Everyone seemed to know their lines, their role and their position in the hierarchy of the high school's dynamic. Ugh, this was so painful. When I walked into my first class and sat down at a desk, the girl sitting behind me stretched her leg forward and put her foot on the chair, "Saved," she said. I moved to the back of the room and sat down fast before someone else did the same thing.

The teacher was running late, on the first day, not a good sign. A group of girls gathered around the girl who had placed her foot on my chair and stared with one set of eyes at me. I was obviously hated at first sight. When the door handle turned, they scattered like rats to find seats.

"I know most of you, but where is Miss O'Connor, Jenna O'Connor?"

"It's Rose," I said quietly.

"Rose O'Connor?"

"No, Jenna Rose." The whole class laughed, declaring in one voice that I was a loser. "My Grandmother is Mrs. O'Connor, she's paying the tuition." Oh my God, I was going to have to tell this woman and the class the story of my pathetic life. I walked up to the front of the room to talk to the teacher in private.

"I live with my grandmother; she's my mother's mother so my last name is different, it's Rose. I'm Jenna Rose."

My face was heating up with embarrassment. I was not off to a good start. The girl at the head of the clique realm let out a laugh when I passed her. When I looked back at her, I caught her nodding to someone in the back of the room. I hurried and sat down before she had another chance to sabotage me.

"Okay, now, anyone else have anything to tell me? Any name changes? Anyone get married over the summer?" This teacher sounded like an insensitive bitch. I hoped the rest of them were better.

It turned out, they were. I only had *IB-Insensitive Bitch*, for homeroom, so I lucked out there, but I was a social outcast with no connections except for Gypsy. I concentrated on studying but still I felt like a remnant of a dying species. That fact was driven home when Mrs. Morrison, the language studies teacher, decided we'd all need to fine-tune our creative writing abilities in preparation for the SATs and college. She gave us, what for most, was an easy assignment. She instructed us to write two memoirs but gave us the semester to finish them, "I want you to do an outline to help you to get your thoughts in order; the first one is due in two weeks. The first is: *What is the worst thing that ever happened to you*, and the second is: *What is the best thing that's ever happened to you*."

I felt invaded all over again. I hadn't lied since the day I left home. It was not something that came naturally. I'd been trying to be the perfect student. I didn't want to be caught in a lie but I lived in fear of everyone here finding out about my past. How was I going to reveal my worst? It would take a whole lot of creativity to disguise it all. I felt the angst set in as I overheard the blondes discussing the assignment in the bathroom.

"Oh, my God." It was Allison speaking, one of the worshippers of Nicole Elliott, the blonde head of the girl clique, the one I'd encountered on my first day here.

"Remember when our chauffeur had an accident and had to be out of work and your parents couldn't find a replacement so they had to drive you to and from school, and they both showed up to pick you up and they had a huge fight in the parking lot? This could be your worst."

"That never happened, Allison. I took the bus across town then."

"No, you didn't."

"I did," Nicole raised her voice. Apparently, Nicole lived on the Upper East Side but attended this school on the West Side for some undisclosed reason. But still she managed to intimidate everyone and was in charge, there was no doubt about it.

"Well, you're so stupid, Allison, you should write about how you're so color blind, you wore two different color shoes to school last year and more than one time."

Shoes were not a part of the dress code. We could wear any kind of shoes we wanted within reason. I think this was a huge mistake on the part of the school because it was another weapon the cool girls had to use against those of us who weren't a part of the inner circle.

It was during my first week when I found Nicole lurking behind my open locker door waiting to pounce. "Where did you get those hideous shoes, at a consignment shop? You're an orphan, right?" She didn't wait for an answer; she really didn't care. Her arrow had hit its target and this was all that mattered to her. It all made me wonder what was hidden inside of her to cause her to be so insanely cruel.

"Oh, yeah, I remember, that was so embarrassing. That's my worst for sure. I'm not color-blind, Nicole, I got up late that morning and the chauffeur was already waiting. My parents weren't home and I was rushing."

"Yeah, but the chauffeur had to come back to school later on to bring you one shoe. It's more stupid than the worst thing."

I didn't need good instincts to know for sure if I wrote even a version of my truth, my worst was going to be worse than anyone else's.

I spent the next week obsessing over the writing assignment. I was having strange dreams. I dreamt they made me read my paper out loud. I was standing in front of the class and it seemed they knew everything. I was uneasy every moment, like my shoes were permanently on the wrong feet, feet that couldn't feel the floor. I supposed I should talk to Dr. G about this during our next session. I hadn't written a word.

The school was small. There was no blending into the background, no hiding when you found yourself perpetually under attack by the self-appointed orchestrator of the social order of things, aka Nicole Elliott and her disciples. Nicole never let up, so it was a shock when Grandmother called me to the phone, "Jenna, there's a Nicole on the phone for you."

"Hello," I spoke barely above a whisper while holding the receiver away from my face in case she bit me through the phone.

"Jenna or is it Jen; what's your name anyway? I didn't have your cell so I had to look this number up."

"It can be either, my name, it's either one." I was nervous, as if the president or someone else with similar status was on the phone. It was unbelievable considering all I'd been through in my life that this girl already that kind of power over me.

"Whatever, okay so, well the reason I'm calling is, well I know you are friends with Gabrielle, Gypsy, I think she calls herself, right?"

"Yeah, so?"

"Well, I'm having a party next Saturday and I don't have her number and I wanted to invite her. You must have it, right? It's not in the school directory, must be unlisted."

I gave her the number and hung up fast without saying goodbye so she didn't hear the angst in my voice. I bet Meghan was just like her when she was young; she was like her now. My wish that I had come here to Grandmother years ago was vanishing. It would be a struggle getting through just one year of this torment.

Thankfully, there were a few nice girls in some of my classes. There was Angela Baldassari, her father worked for the Italian Consulate. She spoke with an Italian accent. She too, was exiled to the outer limits of Nicole's circle. She was the new student last year, and now I was the "it" girl. Angela wouldn't dare be my friend. She'd talk to me for a minute before a class started but only if it was a class Nicole or one of her informants weren't in. High school was as corrupt as any government. The administration seemed clueless. Every Friday morning, the head mistress held a meeting with the entire student body. Every week she told us how proud she was of the fact: *there's no bullying taking place within these walls.* Denial? Blindness to what's going on, or was it what Gypsy claimed it to be, *the Elliott family donates a big chunk of change to the school every year; the headmistress won't ever say anything about Nicole's behavior. She knows about it, believe me but she cares more about what the board of trustees thinks than a bunch of persecuted kids. All anyone here cares about is money.*

It was worse than the high school drama on T.V.-the script and stories had to come from somewhere.

Chapter Fifteen

I was in the school cafeteria when Gypsy found me. It had been weeks since I'd last seen her. I was still the new girl with few social resources. I hadn't earned a passport to the cool girl's table or anyone else's table either. I sat in leper-like fashion on the outskirts of the cafeteria at the rarely used table near the kitchen. Its function, before I placed myself there, was as a way station between the cook and the serving staff.

"What are you doing this afternoon?" Gypsy asked in her usual breathless tone. We were not in any classes together so she'd escaped the worst/best assignment.

"I have math then history; what else would I be doing?"

"Cut and come with me; I have a photo shoot for Fashion Week. C'mon it'll be fun, besides cuts are expected. You're a senior, seniors have privileges."

It was tempting. I was not sure I wanted to go. I hadn't told Gypsy my story yet, although she'd probably guessed most of it already. She seemed to know everything. I didn't know how to tell her I was ashamed and kind of afraid to be around a photographer.

"C'mon Jenna, I want to show you how I work. You'll love it, c'mon."

I couldn't believe it when I heard myself say, "Okay, but I hope I don't get in trouble."

"Here's a note from your grandmother, just in case." Gypsy handed me an envelope with fancy lace trim.

"Oh, no, I'm not going to forge my grandmother's handwriting. No way"

"Suit yourself." Gypsy shrugged. "I'll wait outside for you."

It was still lunchtime when I moved easily out of the building. Gypsy was in front of the school leaning against the bricks smoking a cigarette. When she saw me coming she dropped it to the ground and stamped it out with the heel of her shoe while rolling her uniform skirt up with one hand and hailing a cab with the other.

"So, did you go to Nicole's party on Saturday?"

"What are you talking about? She'd never invite me to one of her parties."

"She called me and asked me for your number."

"I hope you didn't give it to her; I guess you didn't because she didn't call."

Nicole Elliott was an even worse human being than I thought she was. Wow, she made up the whole scenario just to make me feel more left out than I already did.

The cab headed downtown and came to a stop in front of a run-down building in So-Ho.

The building was rickety and covered in peeling paint. The doorknob was wobbly; there was no doorman or elevator. After we were buzzed in, we climbed the wooden steps to the third floor and opened the curtained double glass doors. I had knots in my stomach, I didn't know why. I expected an ornate, pristine Hollywood post-modern environment but this place was shabby.

"Gypsy, this place is creepy. Are you sure this is the right place?"

"Geez, Jenna, don't you think I know where I'm going? They don't do photo shoots at the Plaza, except for commercials, of course. This is magazine stuff, low key. Relax!"

We were ushered by a gum-chewing receptionist into a large white space with creaking floors. The photographer was busy adjusting high-tech lighting equipment, and then nodded briefly in our direction. Gypsy left the room to change her clothes and have her makeup done. I stood in the corner, fidgeting with my hands. It seemed like hours had passed. There was no place to sit. I shifted from one foot to the other before plopping myself down on the floor. I leaned my back against the wall. The photographer looked over at me, turned away and then turned back and narrowed his eyes. He kept looking at me, making me nervous. Maybe he'd seen me on that site. Oh my God, what should I do? I stayed seated and looked down on the floor. When I looked up again, he gave me a slight wave. He was grinning, he knew, I knew he knew. He recognized me, I could feel it. I couldn't breathe, but all I was doing was breathing. *Calm down*, I told myself. How was it possible? *Think, Jenna! How old was I when the last picture was taken…thirteen.?* How could my father have posted that picture? But I looked so different now than I did back then. I was almost eighteen. Still, he kept looking at me.

Gypsy entered looking transformed and ten years older wearing heavy makeup and sophisticated clothing. She unknowingly saved my day. I stood and moved to the farthest corner of the room while the photographer positioned Gypsy in place. I was still not breathing normally. The room was getting hotter and the lights were getting brighter as the orders started spewing out of the photographer's mouth, "Good, move, turn now, stop…" A beam of light shone, feeling more intense than a thousand suns in my eyes. I felt hot; I felt cold; I was going to throw up. The photographer's voice was now my father's, *C'mon, Jenna, one more shot, pull your legs up, roll on your side, now sit up, pull your legs up again, no- not like that…*I could hear him clearly. The light was suddenly turned on me. Panic rose up from my throat into my head and I felt myself fall to the floor. When I opened my eyes, I was still on the floor; it wasn't a dream. I tried to get up. I had to get out of here. I'd hit the side of my head, I could feel it throbbing. I lay back down on the floor and closed my eyes and then opened them again, trying to focus. Gypsy was hovering.

"What the hell happened to you?" She looked at me and then over at the photographer.

"Justin, you jerk, why did you turn the lights on her?" He waved her off with his hand without looking. "Just playing around, geez what a drama queen."

"Stay here on the floor, Jenna; I called 911, they're on their way. I called your grandmother too. Sorry about this."

The paramedics arrived in what seemed like seconds later. I was dizzy but told them, "I'm okay." It didn't matter, they insisted on taking me to the Emergency Department of N.Y.U. I was unsteady on my feet but walked down the three flights of stairs with the help of the two paramedics. There was an ambulance on the street, a police car and a crowd. It was a circus. A thread had come loose and I was beginning to unravel.

The Emergency Department was packed. I was moved onto a stretcher and then shoved in a corner. Corners seemed to be my new place in the social order. I saw Grandmother approaching. She was with a man I'd never seen before. He turned out to be her attorney, Mr. Stanton. He and Grandmother left together for the nurse's station. It took an hour for them to find my record even though I'd barely been there an hour. Then it took another hour for the nurse to come take blood. I held out my arm for her to insert the needle but stayed lying on my side facing the wall. I felt myself tighten. I wanted to curl myself up, like a dead worm. I couldn't face anyone. I was hit by a tiredness I'd never felt before. When the nurse finished she came around the stretcher to face me. "Would you like to sign an organ donor card?"

"Sure, take whatever you want," I answered with my face buried in the pillow.

"She only fainted, for Christ sake." Gypsy jumped up out of the chair on the other side of the stretcher where she'd been lounging. "C'mon, Jenna, you better get out of here before they take a kidney." She turned back to the nurse. "I'm pretty sure you have to be at least eighteen to sign a donor card; check the chart, she's only seventeen."

"I have to ask, it's my job." The nurse left, pulling the curtain behind her.

Several hours later, everything came back as normal. Normal? What was normal, anyway?

They couldn't detect my invisible bruises so I was sent home. It was nearly 7 p.m., Grandmother, Gypsy and I slumped like a collective bundled heap into Grandmother's car and the driver headed home. Mr. Stanton was left on the curb.

Chapter Sixteen

My senior privilege of one afternoon morphed into three days off from school. I didn't tell anyone what happened. I couldn't, I was not sure myself. If I did tell, what would I say? That I imagined Gypsy's photographer recognized me; I imagined he was part of my father's world? Or that Gypsy's photographer knew the Internet me, the *Teasing Tot?* I supposed this was now my new worst experience. I couldn't write this, it may not even be true. It may only be my worst fears manifesting themselves in my fantasy life. I knew Gypsy suspected something. She didn't ask me anything but she looked at me suspiciously with those piercing copper eyes. On top of all of this, the worst/best essay outline was looming menacingly overhead. I needed to figure out a contingency plan or story. Memories of Jude flooded over me; maybe I should have gone with him, maybe running away was the better plan, better than all this angst. Maybe I shouldn't have called the cops. Maybe I ruined his life too.

I couldn't sleep. I suppressed all those feelings for all those years. I tried to avoid thinking about what my father was really doing, and now it was all I thought about. Even though I had lost myself in the world of literary characters, a part of me had to know what the picture taking really meant. It lurked in the shadows. I'd been in denial, there was no denying it now. What if the photographer did recognize me? I may be on a website I knew nothing about. I may be a *teasing tot*, whatever that meant. I stayed awake for hours mulling it all over, trying to figure out what to do. I remembered Meghan saying we would change our names. I'd do that, I'd change my name as soon as I turned eighteen.

I went to my desk to make a list:

Write the worst essay/ keep it vague
Tell Grandmother the rest of the story
Then tell it to Dr. G.
Then tell it to Gypsy
Do college apps

I added some frivolous items to try to lighten my mood:
Turn 18
Shop for a coat

But then I remembered what was looming on the horizon:
Be brave and go to court, if I have to
Get rid of Jenna Rose

The burden of all this felt like a weight, I was exhausted. When I woke up, I was still at my desk and Grandmother was standing over me. "I knocked so loud on the door and when you didn't answer I was worried and came in. Jenna, what does this mean?" She asked pointing to the last item on my list. "You weren't thinking of doing something to yourself, were you?" She was wiping her eyes.

"No, that's not what it means; I only want to change my name. Maybe use yours."

"Oh." She sighed and sat down on the bed. "What a relief; now what about these?" She was pointing to the first bunch of stuff on the list.

I looked up at her, then put my head back down on my folded arms and began to tell her. I started with the essay assignment, about overhearing my classmate's tragic tales and how I may have to expose myself, put myself out there on display for everyone to scrutinize and judge. I felt myself tense up; my skin tightened and my face reddened. "There's something else, a website called, *Teasing Tots.* My father may have put pictures of me on there. I imagined the photographer at Gypsy's photo shoot recognized me. Maybe he did, but I was a lot younger, I looked different then. Maybe he didn't, maybe I'm losing it. Maybe I should still be home-schooled; if it's not too late to do that, is it?"

"Jenna, you can't hide from the world, you didn't do anything wrong, you have nothing to be ashamed of. I know about the site. I had hoped you would never need to know. It's being investigated. The site is shut down, but I don't know if he put pictures of you on there. There are a lot of children on it, apparently. There's no need to be worrying about what may or may not be true. Let's talk about school. First of all, you don't have to reveal anything to your teachers, your classmates or anyone else if you don't want to. I would advise you not to let these authority figures intimidate you. Most of your classmates you probably won't ever see again after this year is over. Why don't you write the assignment in a different way, talk about being home-schooled, what it was like; avoid talking about your father altogether. He doesn't deserve attention anyway. The truth doesn't always have to be told, you know, except, of course, in a court of law."

She hesitated for a minute. I sucked in my breath, anticipating some more shattering news.

"Speaking of court, I want to talk to you about setting up an appointment with Mr. Stanton, my attorney. I've been keeping him in the loop about what's been going on. Remember I called him that day? He's been looking into things. He contacted an investigator who works for the Lake County, California Police Department in their Crimes Against Children Division. I didn't want you to know unless it was absolutely necessary. I'm sorry it happened this way. I didn't know how to tell you. I had hoped to avoid telling you forever. We need to get this all over with; the authorities need to hear from you. You have to tell them what you remember."

I guess Dr. G had been serious about not discussing our sessions with Grandmother. After all, she was the first one to tell me about the *Teasing Tots* site. I was not telling Grandmother this, I'd caused enough problems. I didn't want to ruin a friendship. But still, I felt hot with riled-up anger, I lashed out, "What else haven't you told me? And for God's sake, can't I call you something else besides, Grandmother? It's so stuffy and formal and pretentious."

Guilt took over where anger reigned a minute ago. I lowered my voice, "Can't I call you Gran or how about Grand?

You rescued me, you are kind of grand. But I thought I was saved when I first got here. I felt so much relief, but then he found me and soon everyone will know all of this. I feel like my old life held onto the hem of the shirt I was wearing when I came here and won't let go no matter how many washes it goes through. I can't escape."

I felt panicky. A tight coldness crept up my arms and I felt my skin tighten again. "Why did he do this to me?" I sobbed. "I feel robbed and ruined. He created a *me* I don't even know. I had no chance to be my own person. You know, the right me. Does that make sense?"

It was more of a statement than a question, but Grandmother/Grand answered anyway, "Your father is a maggot, sorry to say."

"Don't be sorry." I laughed through my tears.

"You are your own person, Jenna. You are stronger than you think. You proved that by having the courage to come here on your own. You are smart, you figured out an escape hatch, now you've found your own safety net. No telling how much you'll be able to accomplish. You need to get all of this behind you so you can get on with the rest of your life. You aren't alone. This time last year, you felt all alone, right?" Her green eyes seemed to have faded since I arrived. I hoped I wasn't a burden, but I was sure I was at least somewhat of a burden.

"Yes, I was all alone." I didn't mention Jude. I kept that part of me hidden, at least for now.

"And another thing, you can call me whatever you want. Keep it clean though," she said laughing while putting her hand on my shoulder. "Now you have people who care about you. Take it one day at a time; I know that's cliché but it's the only way to get through this kind of trauma. Don't be so afraid to get it all out. No one is judging you."

"I'm trying, I just feel sad all of the time. I don't want to, but I do. I want to forget but it all keeps coming back to find me."

"I know, Jenna, but this won't last forever. Anyone who doesn't understand you didn't do anything wrong isn't worth being around anyway. You might try talking to Gabrielle about some of this; you'll be surprised to find out she understands. She's been through some abandonment of her own. She's spent some time here with me over the years. Her mother leaves her alone a lot."

"Okay, I will, thanks," I said but I was not ready to trust Gypsy with the sordid facts of my life. But I agreed to it because I didn't want to talk to Grandmother about it anymore either. I pretended I was feeling better just to avoid going on and on about the same unsolvable problem.

"When is the essay outline due?" Grand said, changing the subject. She was so good at doing that.

"Next week, first it's the outline for the worst topic. It has to be five pages minimum. Then the following week, the best topic outline is due."

"Hmm! Do it the night before; I always work better under pressure."

I excused myself and went to my room to mull things over. It would be a lie to write that the worst thing I'd ever experienced was being home-schooled. It was actually the only good thing in my life back then. I could write about the trauma of having to call the cops on the only friend I had at the time. But that would further sabotage my social status as an outcast. The best essay would be easy; I could write about finding Grand and Gypsy, how it was like finding nuggets of gold in a pile of mud. I grabbed a pen and began writing a work of fiction:

In order to effectively write an essay regarding the worst experience of my life, I need to seriously dissect the experiences I've endured year by year; I need to evaluate them as to the magnitude of the pain they've caused as well as the experience itself and its after effects. I need to figure out if the experience caused or will cause lasting damage, if I've recovered, if I need help dealing with it and if I will need help in the future.

Well, the outline was shaping up nicely. It sure was vague, if only I knew what I was writing about. I needed more time. I supposed I could write about starting school in my senior year, in a school where everyone was already form-fitted into the space they occupied and I was left swimming around in open water. This would really piss them off; give them more freak fuel.

Chapter Seventeen

When I returned to school on Monday, Mrs. Morrison announced our "worst/best essay" assignment was being cancelled. She stammered when she said she'd *rethought the assignment and had decided an academic topic would be more suitable.* If the character, Mrs. Havisham from Charles Dickens' *Great Expectations* could step off of the page, I envisioned her looking like Mrs. Morrison. She was anorexic thin, and her eyes were encased in deep, dark circles. She wore a dress that didn't fit and gave off the appearance of a bygone era. Her shoes were sturdy with sensible heels. If you got close enough, you could smell her fruity perfume and surprisingly a hint of cigarette smoke. It was almost tolerable now. Her change of assignment made me feel like the gods (and goddesses) were finally on my side and the *one day at a time* idea of Grand's was sounding plausible after all. I'd spent two weeks worrying for nothing. I even started the stupid outline.

Nicole and her disciple, Allison, came into the bathroom and were discussing the matter. I was already in the first stall, they didn't notice; I stood by the door listening.

"That weirdo, Mrs. Morrison had to cancel the assignment because parents called to complain," Nicole announced with authority.

"Really, why would they do that?" I was picturing Allison looking up at Nicole with adoring eyes. Made me sick.

"Well, my mother's the president of the Parent's Association," *Of course she was*, I thought to myself, "and she said one of the mother's is a high-powered attorney in some Park Avenue law firm."

"So?" Allison interrupts.

"So, dummy, she said asking students to write personal stuff like their worst experiences is a violation of their privacy."

I turned around and leaned my back onto the stall door and wondered if it was my grandmother who made the call. I wasn't going to ask her though; I was going to forget this. Whatever assignment Mrs. Morrison was planning now was going to be a breeze compared to the last one. Bring it on; I thought smiling.

Nicole and Allison lingered in the bathroom, so I was stuck. I didn't want to face them. Dealing with Nicole was like chronic fatigue.

"If you think about it, Allison, there are probably a ton of kids here with secrets; like the new girl, Jenna, for example, whoever heard of starting a new school in your senior year? She's got to be hiding something; maybe she had a baby and had to leave her old school or maybe she's a *Juvie* or maybe she was in rehab. Something is off with her, don't you think?"

"Yeah, probably that girl Gypsy knows."

Wasn't there enough to talk about in the city of New York without having to make shit up about people you didn't know anything about? Going to an all-girls school in the city didn't offer much opportunity to participate in sports. We ran in the park, swam in the school's pool, but the real sport was target practice. Nicole could win an Olympic medal for her bulls' eye accuracy. The worst/best assignment woe had now given way to a new angst.

I over stayed my allotted bathroom break and had only a minute to get to my locker before my next class. When I turned the corner, I saw Nicole confronting Gypsy. She didn't waste any time.

"So, what's up with your new BFF Jenna? What's she doing here, living with her grandmother? What kid moves in with their grandmother anyway? Is she an orphan, a druggie? What's she hiding? You must know something."

"I don't know, Nicole. What are you hiding? Must be something in that fucked up bitchy head of yours to make you so mean. Too bad, with all those buckets of money your parents have, they couldn't have paid somebody to turn you into a human being!"

Gypsy just walked away. She didn't even raise her voice; she said it all like she'd been rehearsing for a decade. It was so spontaneous; she didn't even know I was within earshot. I slid my back along the lockers in the hall and slipped unnoticed into my next class.

"Everything okay?" Grand turned to look at me when I came into the kitchen after school. I hooked the handle of my backpack on the corner of the kitchen chair, sat down at the table and let out a sigh.

"Mrs. Morrison cancelled the assignment, you know the one I was worrying about."

Grand turned around again, wiped her hands on the towel tucked into her apron and looked at me. "Really, why did she do that?"

"Well, according to Nicole Elliott, the worlds authority on everything, somebody's lawyer mother complained about rights to privacy being invaded or something."

"Nicole Elliott, Savannah Elliott's daughter?"

"Yeah, I guess so; why, do you know her?"

"Yes, I know her; I wouldn't be surprised if she was the one who called the school; a whole lot of skeletons in that closet," Grand whispered turning back to the stove.

"Now, how about the coat you're going to be needing? Any ideas what kind you might want? She changed the subject with rapid fire precision, again.

As fascinated as I was with the possibility of Nicole Elliott having a past as bad or worse than mine was, the idea of coat shopping surpassed even that. I never had a coat; I'd had jackets and sweaters but never a coat. I had no idea what to get. I'd have to ask the mistress of fashion, Gypsy. I hadn't seen much of her lately; after school, she rushed off to photo shoots in different parts of the city. Fashion week would be over on Friday and then things would be back to the way they were.

Chapter Eighteen

I'd overslept, probably missed all of my morning classes. I got up, pulled the curtains and saw my first snowfall. It looked like the clouds had descended down to earth and had landed lightly on the surface. It was early though and the snow was untouched; not a snow shovel or a plow was anywhere in sight. It was still snowing lightly, quietly and feathery. It looked surreal. I wanted to go out and put virginal footprints on the landscape. But reality set in, I didn't have a coat; I'd have to wear one of Grand's. I was already enough of an alien at school without showing up, looking like a dreck, in my grandmother's coat. There would be no coming back from this with Nicole.

Grand sat at her desk writing checks. No matter what time I got up, she was already awake, showered and dressed. I wondered if she slept at all.

"Did you see the snow?" I asked, embarrassed by my childish enthusiasm.

"Sure did."

"I still don't have a coat or boots; how will I go to school today?"

I continually worried about fitting in. I didn't, and I won't ever fit in, this was a fact and I wasn't sure why I cared at all. I didn't even like my classmates. This must be a stage of teenage development. After I was finished with this dreadful year, I'd never see any of these people again. Yet, now all I wanted was for them to like me. Crazy!

"No school today. The new mayor has exercised his authority and has shut down the city. But it will warm up later and the stores will open. By the time that happens the sidewalks will be mostly cleared and you can take the subway downtown or go over to Bloomingdale for a down coat. Better consult Gypsy, she'll be up to date on the latest styles."

Gypsy was unavailable, nowhere in sight and she wasn't responding to texts so Grand called her driver and we headed across town to Bloomingdales. He parked in a row of other black cars which were lined up in front of the store on Third Avenue.

A Gypsy consult wasn't necessary because the coat department was a sea of black. It looked like puffed up Orcas had beached themselves on hangers. I tried on the only colorful coat I could find. It was isolated on a rack in the corner near the fitting room, as if being punished for daring to be different. I loved it, it was me. It was a royal blue wool coat with a black belt.

"Oh, you can't wear that to school," the saleslady informed me. "They'll make fun of you, dear. You'd better get one of these," she said handing me an Orca. I looked like a fat missionary.

Grand cheered me up by insisting I get the blue one too. "For weekends and dinners out," as she put it.

The heaven-sent snow had now become an ugly gray mass. Navigating the streets for an amateur like me was tedious especially in UGG boots. My feet felt like alien life forms had attached themselves by artificial means to the bottom of my legs. They were hideous but everyone was wearing them proudly like they were Valentino originals.

The melting snow piled up on every curb making it impossible to pass by without acquiring a boot full of wet slush. I saw Gypsy climb a mound of snow with ease as she hailed a cab to school. I hadn't seen her in a while; I was starting to think I did something wrong or if she'd joined the ranks of the Nicole Elliott crowd after all. She used to stop by to get me every morning and we would go to school together. I made my own way there and found her in the cafeteria, sitting alone, texting someone.

"What's up? I haven't seen much of you lately."

I was sorry I asked, for the next twenty minutes, she went on and on about her new boyfriend. He was much older, nearly twenty-seven and a photographic journalist on top of that. I didn't like him already. His name was James, not Jim or Jimmy. It was James this and James that.

"Isn't he a little old for you?" She just shot me one of her classic, *give me a break, I know what I'm doing,* looks. I had a feeling my best friend status was dwindling. I was being deleted, again.

Chapter Nineteen

Christmas in New York had been a magical one. Grand took me to see *The Nutcracker* and then to a trendy restaurant. It was so loud Grand couldn't hear a word I said. We ate dinner in silence while searching around for the celebrities we had heard frequented the place. I turned eighteen in early December. For my birthday, Grand had given me a white German Shepherd puppy. She was five months old now. Monks from upstate had trained her. Her name was Gracie. When she gave her to me, Grand said, *Now, you don't have to walk the streets alone.* Dr. G gave me a journal and Gypsy didn't show up; Meghan didn't call either. It was disappointing but this birthday had been far better than any other so I couldn't really complain.

The Christmas ambiance melted away like a fast-moving snowstorm. It had been enchanting and I wanted the season to last forever. But now, a new year had blown in hard with the cold winter wind. It was a new year all right but the old stuff still lingered.

"We have an appointment with my attorney, Mr. Stanton, tomorrow after school," Grand reminded me as if I could forget.

I'd expected to go home and change before meeting with the attorney, but I saw Grand's car when I walked out of school. Nicole Elliott followed close behind. I seemed to be her mission or maybe her prey. She tossed her blonde hair up and over her shoulder with her right hand while turning to her left to whisper something to Allison. I could see her pointing toward Grand's car through the tinted window as we pulled away. I wondered what ammo she was gathering up to fire at me this time. It was Thursday, since we had Friday and Monday off for a February mini break, Nicole would have some extra time to concoct a Jenna rumor.

The receptionist in the law offices saw us stepping out of the elevator and rushed to open the door. "Nice to see you, Mrs. O'Connor; Mr. Stanton is expecting you, you may go right in." Grand didn't respond, nor did she introduce me to the woman, which was weird and unlike her. We followed her into an inner hallway and through the large double door where Mr. Stanton's name appeared under the name, O'Connor.

Mr. Stanton greeted me first; he held both of my hands in his. His hands stayed placed on top of mine like they were waiting instruction. He was in his early fifties, maybe. His hair was black with white strands running through it. Skunk came to mind; it was way too long, for his age. He kept nervously pushing it away from his eyes. He murmured rather than spoke; this seemed to be an odd trait for a lawyer to have. I didn't know what his role was going to be in this case but there was something about him I didn't trust. Call it gut.

The meeting lasted barely a half an hour, more of a meet and greet, similar to the "go-sees" Gypsy had for her modeling gigs. But this was going to be the gig of a lifetime. Mr. Stanton didn't ask me many questions, which was a relief, but strange. Maybe he was just trying to lull me into a comfortable and cozy state of mind before he launched his attack. The whole thing seemed like a waste of time.

I was in my room with Gracie when I heard Grand on the phone in the hallway. When I heard her hang up, I got up and went to the kitchen where she was having tea. She looked upset.

"What's up?"

"Oh, it's just business."

"You can tell me, I tell you stuff." I looked at her raising my eyebrows; it was how she always looked at me when she was fishing for info.

"Mr. Stanton transferred to the California office. He took care of all of my business here in New York. He didn't say a word about it, he's just leaving. It's strange."

"I never liked that stony settlement."

"That what?" she asked laughing.

"Oh, well that's what his name means. Sometimes I look stuff up, like names. It can tell you a lot about a person. Maybe names aren't all that random. Like Dr. G, for example, her name means, "Commander of an army." That was what it was going to take to bring my down my father, I didn't say it though.

"You're a funny girl-young lady, Jenna. That's clever and probably quite accurate. I don't know what's going on but Mr. Stanton did seem distracted and up to something. I guess it was the move to California essentially behind my back. It's an odd move for him; he was a fervent New Yorker."

I followed Grand over to the stove. I leaned my elbow on the counter while putting my head forward to sniff the cookie aroma coming out of the oven. Valentine's Day was a day away and Grand was preparing heart shaped cookies. Not sure why, it was just the two of us. I guess she was just trying to make my life as festive as possible to keep my mind off of the trial I'd be facing soon. I would be called to testify, that was a given. It all hovered in the air like an odor that couldn't be sprayed out.

Chapter Twenty

When SATs were finally over, Grand and I decided it may be best to defer college for at least a semester after the ordeal of the trial was behind me. Grand had a new lawyer, Camille De Marco. She agreed a name change was a good idea. This way, I could apply to college under my new name, distancing myself from my father, psychologically at least.

Camille was a former New York State prosecutor from Long Island. She was now general counsel in Grandfather's old firm. She barely stood five feet, but was a firecracker according to Grand. Her dark red hair, angelic blue eyes and demure smile led people to underestimate her.

Grand told me after seeing her in action, "She can cut the witness to the quick before he knows what hit him." I wasn't sure what that meant but I felt better having her on my side. She'd come to court with me if and when I was called along with Dr. G and Grand. I always hoped Gypsy would come too, although I hadn't told her much. She'd been going on and on about getting engaged to James on Valentine's Day. I secretly hoped it wouldn't happen.

But, sure enough, on the night of Valentine's Day, the doorbell rang. When I opened it, Gypsy shoved her left hand in my face. The ring was a ridiculously large antique emerald cut yellow diamond surrounded by white diamond chips. Gypsy was dressed up.

"Must be ten carats," I said, not having a clue what I was talking about.

"Close but only six," she answered while jumping and nearly cracking her head on the ceiling in the doorway.

"So where did he take you?"

"Oh, we went to the Valentine's Day dance at school. It was kind of nice, considering."

There was a strong tug in the pit of my stomach. I couldn't imagine Gypsy willingly attending a school function in my worst nightmare scenario. But here she was telling me all about it. I felt the gravitational pull of that distant planet suddenly intensify, where I'd been exiled since school started. I knew all about the dance. Our school had invited several private boys' schools to participate. I did wonder about it; I wondered if the boys would be uncorrupted by Nicole Elliott. I wondered if any of them would have paid attention to me. I wondered but wouldn't dare take the chance. I figured Nicole would find a way to sabotage me even if I were only appearing to have a good time. Bad enough I had to endure her during regular school hours, there was no way I'd give her extracurricular time to screw me over.

"Let's go show Grand your ring; what did Adele say?"

"Adele doesn't know. She's traveling and doesn't like me to call her unless it's an emergency."

It felt strange to be the only one to know about this important step in someone's life. But then I realized I wasn't the first to know, everyone who was at the dance knew before me, before any of us. I may be lost but Gypsy was more adrift than I was. She had no guidance or anyone who seemed to care. It was no wonder she latched on to her long, dead grandmother and now onto a much, too much older guy. At least I had the sense not to follow Jude into the ominous life he was barreling toward. Was I just wimping out or was I smarter than this? Maybe if I didn't have a grandmother, I wouldn't have had hope and I would have followed that path too. I didn't want to think about Jude and how I was the one who made his call for help. I only hope it turned out that way; I was afraid to know how it turned out, really afraid.

Grand was shockingly supportive as she "oohed and ahhed" over Gypsy's ring. I couldn't believe my ears.

Gypsy, after her mission was accomplished, went off to meet James. Adele's apathy was what fueled Gypsy's rebellion.

At least this was my amateur psychological assessment. She spent most nights at James' apartment in the West Village. Most mornings, she was late for school. After she left, I asked Grand why she seemed so happy for her.

"I've lived long enough to know when someone's heart is made up, their mind won't be changed. They have to get it all out of their system. It's not my place to be the voice of doom. I'd rather let her know I'll always be supportive. Even after the train wreck, she'll know this is a place she can fall. By the way, it's going to be getting a little noisy around here; I bought the apartment next door and the walls between here and there have to come down."

Chapter Twenty-One

Every day, carpenters and painters and occasionally an architect graced us with their presence at 8 a.m. After a few weeks, Gracie got used to them and stopped barking. She growled lightly in their direction but barely lifted her head. Between the dust inside and the cold outside, I had perpetual laryngitis.

The November snowfall had been the only winter storm so far, but the wind kept up all season. It was ferociously cold and the sting bit into my face. It felt like pine needles had dislodged from the trees in the park and had regrouped on my cheeks. Even my eyes were cold. My California raised body was not adjusting well to the Northeast climate.

"It will be spring soon," Grand reassured me.

But spring didn't come until mid-May. It lasted a week and then it was hot. Suddenly it was two weeks until graduation. I hadn't heard from Meghan since that dreadful day when I told her I'd be staying here in New York. She'd given birth to me; I'd assumed she'd remember I'd turned eighteen and would be graduating from high school this June.

"No prophet is without honor except in his own place," Grand told me when she saw me moping. "It's a quote from the bible, Matthew 13:57."

"I don't get it."

"Well, even Jesus was shunned by the people in his hometown. They remembered him as the carpenter's son. So, if you put it into a modern perspective, in your own place, depending of course, on the way you were raised and by whom, the narrow-minded and the holier than thou relatives are unlikely to ever honor you justly or fairly, no matter what you accomplish."

"It makes sense, I guess, but still I want my mother to be proud of me, how well I'm doing, how much I've overcome, something. But it seems she isn't proud of any of those things. I'm not going to dwell on it."

"Good, it's her loss."

I picked up Gracie's leash and attached it to her collar. I had one hand on the doorknob I turned toward Grand. "I have an appointment with Dr. G; I'm taking Gracie with me."

"I'm going to a charity dinner tonight, I won't be late."

"K," I yelled back. I was already out the door.

Gracie brushed herself protectively against me as the elevator filled with fellow tenants. We exited six floors down; Dr. G's apartment/office was in the corner. Only two apartments were on this floor. The other tenant only used his apartment on the rare occasions he came into town to see his latest mistress. It was one of the tidbits I overheard Dr. G tell Grand when I was hanging around the closed door hoping to hear some secret, cloak and dagger information about myself.

The apartment door was unlocked; she was expecting me. The entry way was wide and held two over-stuffed dark leather chairs which sat like two gangsters facing the door as if they were hired to do a pre-evaluation of Dr. G's patients. They made me nervous. Chairs were making me nervous now. The lighting in here was dim and the faint smell of incense made me feel like I was about to have a tarot card reading. Dr. G unlocked the inner door and pointed to the sofa where for weeks and weeks I'd sat and had slowly begun to weave the bits of anecdotes which made up the story of my life, into a well-formed narrative. I didn't think any of it was a life. I was only living now for the first time. I sensed though, that I was being groomed for court.

Gracie settled herself on the floor by my feet, as the session wound down, she stood up, stretched a few times and then put her head on my knee.

"She's a good therapy dog; you know, I can officially designate her as one. Then she can travel to California with you in the cabin of the plane. I think that might be a good idea."

I didn't answer, my eyes met hers in a long stare before I looked down at Gracie and attached her leash to her collar. It was all I needed now, a therapy dog, wearing a therapy jacket signaling to the world her owner was flawed. People wouldn't be stopping to admire Gracie for her beauty like they did now. Instead, they would shy away from petting her for fear they would interrupt her from her task of coming to the aid of her somehow defective charge—me! I felt anger rising up but I said nothing to Dr. G, not even goodbye before heading out the door and east toward Central Park.

It was nearing dinnertime. Moms and nannies were pushing strollers out through the entrance to the park in a mass suppertime exodus. Gracie and I headed for one of the open fields. I unleashed her and reached for the tennis ball in my pocket. My first throw was impressive giving Gracie a good run. She returned to my side and dropped the ball at my feet. The second throw rendered the first one a fluke; it flew off to the side. I turned to keep Gracie in my line of vision when I saw a creepy homeless guy coming near. Gracie dropped the ball and seemed to fly to me like a mythical winged white beast. Her tail was between her legs, her head was down and she was growling as the man got closer.

"Got any spare change, Miss? I need something to eat." He was smiling at me like he knew me. I leashed Gracie, handed him a dollar and broke into a run out of the park. Maybe he recognized me. I had that sick feeling again. Would it ever be over? *Be sensible,* I told myself, how could a homeless person have access to that website? Maybe he could, but it was more likely I was turning into a paranoid mess.

Once out of the park, I bent down and patted Gracie on the head. This was a new phenomenon for me, this someone-something always being around to put their foot/paw out to block the doorway to my demise. Grand was still home when I returned. "How come you're home so early?"

"I decided not to go; I'm feeling tired tonight." She looked tired. It scared me.

"You're back early, did something happen?"

Grand seemed to have a sixth sense or maybe radar in the back of her head that allowed her to pick up on the slightest out of the ordinary event taking place either near or far. I thought it was best to come clean. I told her about the homeless guy in the park and Gracie coming to the rescue.

"You are on the verge of having more stories to tell than I do."

"I like yours better."

In all the stories Grand told me, she rarely mentioned her mother except to say, *the aunts blamed her for leaving her five children motherless.* Aunt Eileen was included in the group. Grand's mother couldn't help dying. All the aunts except for one were spinsters; they blamed their sister for having sex too often resulting in too many kids in too short a time. They believed that Grand's mother died because *God punished her.* It didn't seem to me, that a religion should be teaching people to think this way. At least Grand's mother loved her children. I couldn't say the same about mine. I was graduating tomorrow and my mother would be a no-show. Wish I could be too, but Grand was making me go.

Adele was a no-show at graduation too. Grand sat with James and a girl he brought with him. I was hoping she was his sister. After the ceremony was over, I pushed through the crowds of beaming parents taking group selfies and made my way to the exit. I stood there waiting for Grand to find me. As much as she wanted a picture of me for the top of the mantle, she knew better than to ask. I saw Gypsy posing with James; the unknown girl was taking the pictures. Gypsy didn't look happy. What I didn't see was Nicole Elliott and her mother coming up behind me.

"Nicole, is this your new little friend?" Mrs. Elliott spoke through an unopened mouth. Her face was so tight she could barely move her lips. She was blonder than Nicole.

"Not a friend, a new classmate. This is Jenna Rose, Mrs. O'Connor's granddaughter."

"Oh," she said holding my hand limply in hers. She didn't let it go.

"Are you Meghan O'Connor's daughter? Is she here?" I didn't answer.

"Aren't you an orphan?" Nicole asked, knowing full well I wasn't.

"Oh, no, I'm sure Meghan is very much alive and off somewhere with some man. Oops, didn't mean to say that out loud." They turned around to leave and bumped into Meghan who was standing behind them listening to the whole exchange.

"Well, if it isn't *Thing One and Thing Two,* out on a day pass, Savannah?"

Nicole and her mother walked off without saying another word. I was stunned; my mother showed up after all. "Meghan why are you here?"

"To see you graduate; I'm not staying though, I don't want another altercation with my mother, but I wanted to be here for you, this once. I thought it was important." Meghan kissed me on both cheeks, handed me an envelope and left me standing there.

Grand found me a few minutes later, "Wow it's crowded, for such a small school. Let's go home." It seemed she missed seeing Meghan altogether and if it weren't for the envelope I would be thinking I dreamt the whole thing.

"Who are *Thing One and Thing Two,* Grand, do you know?"

"Didn't you ever read, *The Cat in The Hat,* when you were little?"

"No."

"I'm sorry to hear that. Well, *Thing One and Thing Two*, are mischief-making characters the cat releases from his hat. It's a book by Dr. Seuss. You should read it. It's never too late." Was it ever too late for things like that or things like a mother-daughter relationship?

Gypsy, James and the unknown girl came over to greet us as we made our way to the waiting car. "Congratulations," James said to me. "This is my friend, Madeline." She nodded unresponsively in my direction.

"What did that troll, Nicole want?" Gypsy asked.

"Nothing, her mother knew mine, I think, it doesn't matter. I'm finished with Nicole Elliott."

The Gypsy/James trio, left to go have lunch and Grand and I were left on our own. I wanted to go home, this was too much of a family scene. Even though Meghan showed up, she didn't have the guts to stick around. I was thankful she showed up but it was hard not to notice all the fathers and mothers and siblings fawning over my classmates.

There wasn't much time to mull over my future. It was early morning on the day after graduation when I found a letter sitting on the edge of the table in the entryway. It was the same mahogany table I had grabbed onto when I'd made my first ungraceful entrance into Grand's life. The letter teetered on the edge like it knew it wasn't welcome. Gypsy must have been here; she had a habit of picking up our mail. Her morning rendezvous when she wasn't shacking up with James was coercing the mailman into handing over our mail as well as hers and Adele's. She routinely threw it haphazardly on the table before presenting herself. It was where I found it, on top of the latest bill from Con-Ed. The return address stated: California, San Francisco to be exact. Unless the government was wishing me a happy graduation, it was a letter from the court summoning me to testify against my father. The time had come; I knew it would, but always hoped it wouldn't. I could tell by looking at the envelope that they'd turned this into a federal case.

PART THREE

Chapter One

"Would you like something to drink?" the flight attendant asked in a voice that seemed nearly out of breath. I could only make out the first letter of her name…L. It peeked out from under the blue sweater she was wearing. She had the worn-out look of someone whose career was winding down. She moved erratically like a broken clock. Maybe today was her last day or maybe it was her first. She was unmarried; her bare left hand held a pad where she wrote down our order. Maybe she was a widow, hired by a sympathetic airline executive. I studied her; something about her was familiar.

"I'd like coffee, please, with cream, no sugar," my grandmother said looking up from her book.

"And I'd like a cappuccino with a dusting of cinnamon and chocolate on top, please."

"I'm sorry but we don't have cappuccino on board," L told me without expression.

"I figured, but you asked me what I'd like and that's what I'd like."

"She'll have an orange juice." Grand turned toward me scowling. "Gabrielle seems to be rubbing off on you. This is not a good time for that to be happening."

The stiff, humorless flight attendant returned with our drinks. After a few seconds, I remembered she was on the flight with Missy, the flight attendant who was on the plane the night I flew from California to New York almost a year ago. Wow! She was like a thread connecting my old life to my new one and back again. I wondered if she'd be able to hold the thread long enough for me to disconnect one life from the other and sever the tie once and for all. I thanked her for the juice and turned to Grand. "So how come you never talk about your siblings?"

"They didn't like people they thought had too much money. They thought having money was sinful and your grandfather and I would never get into heaven," Grand shrugged. "I distanced myself from them. Your grandfather worked very hard, and I worked hard. We were successful. People used to come to the United States from all over the world looking for the "pot of gold" at the rainbow's end. If they happened to find it, sometimes those who weren't as fortunate or as clever would ostracize them. My siblings said we were just lucky. Luck played a small part, but your grandfather took risks. He was working when other people were sleeping or playing. I got tired of apologizing. They judged me without having any idea what my life was really like. It was hard, but I cut them off." She turned back to her book and didn't tell me why or how her life had been so hard.

The pilot's voice broke free of the static-filled overhead speaker and gave God-like instructions to the flight attendants in preparation for take-off. Our flight attendant, L, strapped herself into the makeshift seat which pulled off the wall like a no-frills Murphy bed. I peeked over the seat in front of me in time to see her kick off her shoes and rub her feet. They looked their part, deep pink on the verge of blistering. They looked like they'd walked across the country several times a day. As Grand would say, *she's not wearing sensible shoes.* Should I tell her? Give her my Gypsy inherited fashion advice, save her from herself? After all, we were connected by the thread, the plane which had carried me back and forth from my old me to my new me.

I daydreamed my way through the next few hours. I assigned life scenarios to my fellow passengers. I thought the man across the aisle was a corporate spy. His tray table was covered with papers; his right arm was placed around them in case someone tried to cheat off of him. Every few minutes, his eyes darted around like he was expecting to be found out. It was all boring and juvenile. I sighed. Grand looked over and put a crinkled tissue in her book to mark her place before returning it to her carryon.

"I'm sorry for not paying attention to you. This is one of those books that rarely comes along. You know the type you cannot put down?"

"It's okay, I'm fine, just nervous, I guess. But why is this a federal case? Do you know?"

"I think it's because of your father's involvement with the Internet photos. That is a federal offense. I think it's considered trafficking. Also, the child he had with him may have been taken across state lines. We don't even know if the woman was her mother. I'm not sure, but Camille will know. Just answer the questions honestly and you'll be just fine. We may be meeting the prosecutor later today. It's going to be okay, I promise."

We were going to be in California for a few weeks. I missed Gypsy and Gracie already. Dr. G had been subpoenaed but I wasn't sure what she could tell them. She couldn't tell them anything I told her without my permission. She was flying out later. I had hoped Gypsy would have joined me but she stayed behind to see that Gracie got off okay. She was returning to the Monks for a few more weeks of training. This was just her excuse; Gypsy needed to keep her eye on James' wandering one. I didn't know why she was marrying him or why he was marrying her either. The date had been set for late September. I was to be the Maid of Honor. I wasn't even excited. I never had a girlfriend before now and it felt like I'd only had her for a few minutes.

The plane jolted and the Flight Attendant lost her balance. "It would just be my father's luck if the plane went down and I couldn't testify." Grand patted my arm and went back to her book. The plane righted itself and we sailed through clearer skies into California airspace.

Chapter Two

The hotel Grand picked out was a new one with an awesome view of the bay and the bridge going over it. It was on the opposite end of San Francisco from the courthouse. Grand wasn't taking any chances I'd bump into either one of my parents. We checked in with the receptionist at the front desk, a girl who looked about my age. A basket on the ledge was overflowing with Milk Bone dog biscuits. I missed Gracie, this was the first time we'd been separated for more than a few hours.

"I reserved several rooms and a suite," Grand told the girl. "I will also be needing the services of a driver who can be on call during my entire stay."

"Yes, Mrs. O'Connor, it's all arranged."

Grand could sure be bossy. She wore her wealth when she needed to. I knew she was expecting Dr. G, but I'd thought she and I would be sharing a room. Our rooms connected through a double-sided door. Hers was a suite with a living room and a dining room. I didn't know why we needed all this space, but I was so tired I didn't ask. I unpacked and left Grand to do the same. The prosecutor was coming to the hotel. We'd spoken on the phone and I gave a preliminary testimony via a Skype kind of thing lawyers used. She was coming by to help me feel at ease, as if that was even possible at this point. I was expected in court in the morning.

I knocked lightly on Grand's door. "I'm so tired, do you think you can cancel the meeting with the prosecutor? I'm not a baby. I don't need to see her before tomorrow. I just want to sleep."

"I understand how you feel but it's their procedure. Let me see if I can cancel. Go take a rest."

I had no doubt Grand would successfully cancel, she was used to getting her way. I was glad she was on my side. I slept, most of the night. I had that same stupid dream where I was hanging on to the side of the boat. It was the same boat in the old dream where Meghan and my father were trying to row in different directions. But in this dream, I fell off and when I finally reached the shore, Grand was there holding a big towel. She wrapped it around me and we walked off together. I didn't look back. It was a nicer dream than the others but it didn't make me feel any better.

The chauffeur was waiting under the awning in the circular driveway outside our hotel when we came through the hotel door. The courthouse was several miles away. Every few feet we found ourselves stopped at a red light. The roads were a schizophrenic maze of trolley tracks and crisscrossing lanes. As we made our way straight down on Market Street, I watched the neighborhoods devolve. Tourists holding shopping bags co-mingled with street people who were carrying all their worldly goods in carts.

"Look at those people."

"There was a time when New York was just as bad as this." Grand turned her head slightly to glance out my window. "It's better now, but things are deteriorating again. Not as bad as this—yet. I guess the weather here is more amenable to living full-time on the street."

I didn't know what she was talking about; I was freezing and it was July. I thought it was going to be warmer here. I had the wrong clothes. I only had a light sweater. It was cold. I should've known, I was from here.

We exited Market Street by driving down a steep hill where government style buildings lined the wide streets. The Federal Courthouse was a tired looking glass building located on an unimpressive side street. The driver pulled up to the sidewalk. The driveway was blocked with large metal studs. A bored security guard sat in front with his nose in a newspaper. He didn't look up in our direction. There were no steps of justice to climb like on *Law and Order*. This courthouse had no grandeur. I hoped there were people inside who knew what they were doing. I had expected to be wowed by an imposing regal structure.

The security line inside the courthouse snaked around the marble entryway. It had a do-it-yourself post 911 impermanent feel to it. No one could enter the inner sanctum of the court without checking all cellphones and electronic equipment. The line was filled with newbie lawyers who walked through the scanner only to be told to start over by removing their belts, keys and coins.

Don't they travel, ever? They seemed new to security. I handed over my cellphone along with Grand's and got two gold numbered coins in return. They could be exchanged at the end of the day for the phones. I watched as the phones were placed into two side-by-side numbered slots. The woman behind me on line asked the guard in a sing-song flirty voice if he wouldn't mind plugging her phone in for just a "teensy while to give it a teensy charge," he answered, "No," in the same sing-song voice.

We were directed to room 101, which was on the second floor for some reason. The judge's assistant, Miss Myer introduced herself before directing us to have a seat on the bench lining the hall outside the courtroom until I was called to testify. Witnesses were not allowed to listen to the testimony of other witnesses on the case. We were an hour early. I sat on my hands to keep them from shaking. The outer hall of the courtroom was an impressive museum quality sea of marble. The floor was white marble, the walls were white marble and the ceiling was marble with an interruption here and there where gold molding was carved into flower shapes which seemed to have been planted ornately in between.

I dreaded seeing my father. I wondered if my mother was testifying. I was a different person now than the one they both knew before. My mother's brief visit to my graduation didn't amount to anything since she'd barely spoken to me, and the envelope she'd handed me only had a card in it—no gift. She had no idea who I was.

I sat for what seemed like hours in silence. I'd been told by the paralegal for the prosecution to expect to testify for at least a week, maybe two.

I heard a voice I recognized coming from the direction of security, it was Camille. She'd been working in the California office. She sat down on the bench and gave me a reassuring pat on the knee. "I'm going to be sitting in the courtroom to see how it's going; don't be nervous. It's going to be okay. We're here to support you."

"She probably knows more about all this than I do, by now," I told Grand after Camille walked away.

"Yes, maybe, but she's bound by law not to discuss the case until the trial is over."

I watched as Camille went through the heavy wooden door, then a court officer came out. We looked over toward him as if on cue and heard him ask for, "Mrs. Stanton, Mrs. Megan Stanton." I felt sick.

"Oh, my God, Grand do you think it's your old lawyer's wife they're calling?"

"No, no, it's just a coincidence."

No one was answering so the court officer, a big burly man in a blue uniform went back through the heavy door and returned a minute later with a female officer who was wearing the same blue uniform. She walked across the hall, opened the door to the lady's room wide enough to stick her head in and called out, "Mrs. Meghan Stanton." Coincidence, I didn't think so and it was confirmed when the door opened wide revealing my mother, looking slightly pregnant.

I opened my mouth in shock and felt tears drip down my face as my mother walked by us. She gave me a sideways glance but didn't stop to talk to me. What could she say? I wished Gypsy was here. She'd know how to handle this and would have done it right on the spot. But she wasn't here. Grand put her arm around my shoulder.

"I don't know what to say about this; it's reckless behavior, and outrageous betrayal and disregard for us both. Stanton, of all people. I knew he was up to something after leaving without a word, but this? This is a sucker punch. I never expected this."

Two hours later, my mother came through the same courtroom door and returned to the lady's room. This time, she avoided all eye contact. Grand got up to follow her just as the court officer emerged again and called my name. I stood up and felt all the blood rush to my head or away from it, I couldn't tell.

"Breathe," Grand told me as we walked arm and arm through the courtroom door.

Chapter Three

The courtroom smelled of freshly applied polyurethane. The floors appeared new and shiny. The center aisle was covered with dark red carpeting. It looked like the runway on that pre-Academy awards show. We walked in, oddly the door was on the right side of the back of the courtroom. We had to walk to the left to go down the center aisle. The first two rows off the center were saved for law enforcement. The Honorable Margaret Silverman sat in the front of the court on a high platform looking regal. Below her sat her assistant and a clerk. The prosecution's table was on the floor level on the right side of the aisle, to the left was the defense table. I could see the back of my father's head. I walked slowly until the judge gestured with a backwards wave for me to "come forward." My feet felt heavy like I was wearing moon boots on earth. Climbing the few steps up to the witness stand was like climbing a hill of molasses. Seeing my mother like that and now my father in this circumstance was too much; I was tired and burdened.

Miss Myer moved toward me and said, "Please remain standing and raise your right hand." There was no bible to swear on like on television. I swore to tell the truth, the whole truth to the best of my ability.

"You may be seated and please state your name for the court."

I was sitting in the witness box on the side of the judge's bench. To my left was the jury. There were eighteen of them, mostly women of diverse ethnic backgrounds. In front of them were computer screens. This was nothing like television court. To my right, in front of me, my father sat between his attorney and a female paralegal. My eyes glanced over in his direction.

He turned toward me, squinted his eyes, raised his right hand and finger gun shot me from across the room. In the frenzy of everyone settling in, no one saw him do this. He immediately turned to his attorney and shook his hand with too much enthusiasm. I willed myself not to look back at him, but my eyes seemed to be in control. I couldn't help myself. My father looked more like a game show host than a defendant. No one else was watching him. He had to be crazy.

Judge Silverman wished me a good morning, and I wished her the same. The prosecutor was conferring with her assistants. I looked up as the courtroom door opened; the room began to fill with people I didn't recognize. But there in the back of the line of arriving spectators were Dr. G and Gypsy. Gypsy waved at me with one hand, while she held tight to Gracie's leash with the other. I let out a nervous laugh when I saw Gracie wearing a therapy jacket. She was a therapy dog whether I wanted her to be one or not. Dr. G got up to leave.

"Why is there a dog in my courtroom?" Judge Silverman peered over the top of her frameless glasses. She pushed her unruly blonde hair back and waited for an answer.

"Therapy dog, Your Honor." Gypsy had no angst about appearances. She was not fazed at all by people's reactions and opinions. She didn't care if it was assumed she was flawed and needed the help of a therapy dog. I was so glad to see her. I felt supported and a bit lighter. No matter what was coming, I was ready, I could handle it. I hoped so, anyway.

"Be seated," the Judge told the arriving visitors, "and keep the dog quiet."

"No problem, Your Honor." Gypsy sat at the end of the pew where Grand was sitting. Gracie lay down on the carpet alongside of Gypsy.

"Miss Cooper, you may inquire."

There were three federal prosecutors, two women and one man. Miss Cooper rose and took long strides across the back of the table up to the lectern on the side of the jury box. She reminded me of a tall stork-like water bird walking in shallow water looking for fish. She had long blonde hair hanging down below her shoulders. Her face was thin and the overall look wasn't working for her. I knew Gypsy would be all over it. I could almost hear her say, *she needs a layer cut or something.* But Miss Cooper was well dressed in a navy-blue suit with a light blue blouse underneath. She adjusted the microphone. "Good morning, Miss Rose."

"Good morning," I said back.

"Speak up and into the microphone so the jury can hear you, please, Miss Rose."

I wished she'd call me, Jenna. I didn't want to be tied to my father. I didn't want to have to reveal my shame to all these strangers.

Miss Cooper's voice had the authoritative tone of a head mistress. The jury seemed to be mesmerized with their eyes collectively fixed on her.

"Miss Rose, how old are you?" I told her and then she asked where I lived and with whom and we went on and on.

"Did you always live with your grandmother?" At that, my father's attorney jumped up from his seat, "Objection to form, Your Honor, leading the witness."

The Judge leaned back to re-read the question the court stenographer had transcribed onto the computer. She looked over at the defense attorney. "Over-ruled, you may continue, Miss Cooper. Miss Rose, answer the question."

"Thank you, Your Honor."

"No, I didn't always live with her."

It didn't end there; I had to tell her why I no longer lived with my parents. I kept it brief.

"My parents are divorced, my father left and my mother went away on business and left me alone so I went to New York to my grandmother's and stayed there." This was not good enough, now she wanted to explore my relationship with Meghan.

"Tell the jury what your relationship with your mother is like." I assumed they had an inkling judging by my mother's current state and name change and also considering the fact she had just testified for over two hours.

"She was hardly ever home." I didn't know what to say. Who cared about this; why was this important? Couldn't she just ask me the questions she really wanted the answers to?

Miss Cooper leaned her hands across the lectern and stared at me intently. "Was your mother involved in your school activities? You know, did she come to see you in school plays, go to parent's night, things like that?"

"I only went to school up to the fourth grade, after I was home-schooled. I went to a real school when I came to New York." I felt tongue tied and confused.

"You didn't go to school?" I assumed it was a question.

"I had tutors."

"Why didn't you go to school, Miss Rose?"

"The school I went to closed and then my father wanted me to be home."

"Why did the school close?"

"I don't know."

"Do you remember the name of the school?"

"No, I don't remember." I had no clue why any of this mattered to anyone, but Miss Cooper held onto the topic like a relentless lion clutching its prey.

"Was it a religious school, do you remember?"

"Yes, I think so."

"Your Honor, at this time, I'd like to present Government Exhibit 122A, the file for the case People vs. Benedict Academy. The school was shut down nine years ago after allegations of abuse were filed with the state. I believe this is the school Miss Rose attended prior to the time it closed down. Permission to publish Government Exhibit 122A, Your Honor?"

"Do I have 122A?" the Judge asked.

"Yes, Your Honor, it's the witness' school record."

"Permission granted." The jurors glanced over at their computer screens with little interest. I had no idea why Miss Cooper was harping on this. I barely remembered attending the school.

"Miss Rose, after your school closed why didn't you go to a different school?"

"My father didn't want me to; he needed me to be home."

"Why was that?"

"Because I was part of his art business." Miss Copper already knew the answer to these questions. This was all a game being played out for the jury. She continued to ask me what my mother did and what kind of art business my father had that required his daughter to be home-schooled. I told her my mother ran an ad agency and my father was a photographer and he took pictures of me.

"Is your father in the courtroom?"

"Yes."

"Please point him out for the jury and describe an article of clothing he is wearing."

I looked at my father, raised my hand and pointed in his direction. "He's there wearing a white shirt and a blue-striped tie."

The Judge turned to face the jurors. "The jury will note the witness has pointed out the defendant, Alan J. Rose. You may continue, Miss Cooper."

"Miss Rose, do you remember ever seeing your father at the school you attended?'

"Yes, sometimes."

"Was he there to pick you up?"

"No, I took the bus home."

"Where in the school do you remember seeing him?"

"Sometimes, I remember I would see him with the principal while I was out on the playground. I don't remember much, it was a long time ago."

"Did you ever come home to an empty house?"

"No."

"Were you ever left alone in your house in California?'

"Yes."

"Tell the jury about those times."

I didn't say anything for a few minutes. I had to think about this; was I left alone? I thought I had been. "When I wasn't in the pink room, I read. If I was left all alone, I had to go into the dark red room."

"You mean your bedroom?"

"No, I mean another room." I was struggling to remember. "It was darker than my room and it was in the attic."

"Tell the jury about the dark red room in the attic."

"It was spooky, full of shadows. I was afraid when I was locked in there."

"How often would you say you were locked in there?"

"Not that many times, but once it was overnight. I think it was haunted; I was afraid."

The whole manner Miss Cooper used to question me was tiring and time consuming. It was court procedure but it seemed like a huge waste of time. I braced myself for more questions when Miss Cooper addressed the Judge, "Permission to approach the witness with Government Exhibit 250, Your Honor?"

Before the Judge had a chance to answer, Gracie let out a loud dog yawn, stood up and stretched her back legs then her front. The courtroom erupted in laughter. The Judge shook her head. "It's 12:35, the dog needs a break. Ladies and Gentlemen of the jury, please return by 2:05 and don't discuss the case."

"All rise," Miss Myer said as the jury exited the courtroom.

I remained standing while Judge Silverman waited a minute before exiting through the same door. I felt dizzy when I walked down the witness stand steps. I looked around the courtroom before leaving; I didn't want to run into either of my parents. My father was out on bail, free to confront me if he wanted to. Camille told me that would be unwise of him, but still, I was afraid. Even now, when he was caught, I was still afraid. The courtroom cleared fast. There was no sign of either Meghan or my father. What was next, I wondered.

I found Grand waiting on the side aisle close to the door; I took her arm and we made our way out. Gypsy was outside with Gracie. Gracie abandoned her good therapy dog behavior and jumped all over me. The driver arrived and we drove off in the direction of the hotel. We didn't have much time but managed to get sandwiches from a local deli. We found benches in a small park by the bay; Gracie needed a break, she lay down on the grass and fell asleep in the sun. It was an escape from the drama of court, at least for a while.

The weather in San Francisco was still cool. I was shivering in my dress and light weight sweater; Gypsy seemed not to mind the chill. She was the first to speak, "You know the lawyer, Miss Cooper?"

"Yes, of course, what about her?"

"She needs a layer cut or something." Gypsy was becoming predictable, and then to prove it she asked, "Is there any place to shop for clothes around here?"

"I'm sure," but frankly I had no idea. I'd never been here before, I'd never even had a girlfriend before her. I guess she didn't remember or maybe believe I wasn't even a real kid before I got to New York. I'd never told her all of it or much of it, really; I'd just assumed she'd guess. She'd know now, but I doubted she'd ask me anything. I was wrong.

"So, you were locked in an attic?" I guess this was a question but I didn't answer. I wasn't sure myself. Maybe I dreamt that part. I felt like a prisoner most of the time but the memory of the attic was a blur. I felt my face redden.

"I don't think we're supposed to discuss the case." I wasn't sure those rules applied to me but it was my excuse for now.

"Oh, right." Gypsy seemed to agree and left it alone.

I was trying to keep my mind on what Grand always said, *live in the now and the future will take care of itself.* But this particular now was scary too. I had a short reprieve from scary and now it was back. Camille wasn't going to answer any of my questions, lawyer's oath, it was an ethical thing. She wouldn't even say who testified. I was the major witness for the prosecution, was all she'd say.

The park's water edge was scenic and peaceful. Grand plopped herself down on a park bench with Dr. G and Camille while Gypsy and I found a spot on a small patch of grass near

Gracie. Gypsy shared her sandwich with the dog; Gracie looked to me for approval before greedily accepting the treat.

"How are you doing?" Gypsy asked with her mouth full.

"Scared, mixed-up, afraid of what's going to happen next, of what they're going to ask me. Do you think they'll show the pictures he took? I only remember the photo shoots taken when I was older. I remember the last one especially. I had just turned thirteen, that one I remember."

"Why is that, Jenna?" Camille interrupted before I could answer. "It's a bit of a drive back; Katherine is tired, we should start back." Grand looked tired, even Gracie looked tired.

"Maybe Grand and the dog should go back to the hotel, Gypsy too, if she wants. I'll be okay with just you there, Camille." I was terrified of something happening to my grandmother.

"I think it's a good idea." Camille left us and went to talk to Grand. I knew she was tired from the trip, the stress of me and the long morning in court. It wasn't over yet."

"Are you sure you're going to be okay? Tomorrow we should go to get your birth certificate. The health administration building is right across the street from the courthouse. I need to rest now, if you're sure."

"Yes, I'll be fine." I really didn't know what it meant to be fine but I had put on my best brave front and hugged her goodbye. "See you in a few hours." Grand, Dr. G, Gypsy and the dog walked in the direction of the hotel. Gracie was the only one who looked back.

I had forgotten about my birth certificate; I'd need it to change my name after the trial was over. My mother had only given Grand my social security number so she could claim me as a dependent if she wanted to. My mother couldn't find my birth certificate. How could you lose the birth certificate of your only child? Guess, I wouldn't be the only child for long. It would be easy to feel diminished if I let myself, but I'd come so far; this would all be in the past soon, never to return, I hoped.

Chapter Four

The judge was already seated when we entered the courtroom. She motioned again with a backward wave for me to come forward and take the stand.

"All rise," Miss Myer instructed as the jury entered the courtroom. They filed one by one into the jury box banging their belongings on the computer screens before taking their seats.

"Good afternoon, ladies and gentlemen."

"Good afternoon," some of them muttered.

"I hope all of you had a good lunch. Miss Rose, you are still under oath. Miss Cooper, you may inquire."

"Permission to put Government Exhibit number 250 on the witness screen but not for the jury, Your Honor?"

"You may."

"Permission to approach the witness?"

The Judge granted permission. Miss Cooper took the evidence of papers and walked her walk toward me. She handed me a photograph, it was already displayed on the computer screen in front of me. "Do you recognize this photograph?"

"Yes."

"Permission to publish Government Exhibit number 250, Your Honor?" Before permission was granted, my father's attorney jumped up and announced, "Government Exhibit 250 is already in evidence, Judge."

"Thank you, Mr. Mulkey, you may inquire, Miss Cooper."

The jury had seen the evidence during another witness' testimony. They seemed unbothered by the picture of a naked little girl with flowers covering her private parts.

"Miss Rose, who is this a picture of?" Miss Cooper was holding the photo in front of me. I saw the exact copy on the computer, double shame.

"It's me," I uttered.

"How do you know that?"

"I recognize my face, I guess."

"Did you ever see this picture before today?"

"No."

"Do you know how old you were at the time this photograph was taken?"

"Maybe three, I'm not sure."

"What is your earliest memory of helping your father practice this art of his?" Miss Cooper returned to the lectern.

"I don't know. I guess I was about five or six; he gave me red liquid. It made me sleepy and when I woke up he wasn't in the room. Sometimes there was a woman there who didn't speak English. She helped him, I guess. It seemed like a dream."

For the next hour, Miss Cooper showed me evidence. There were pictures of people I didn't know; they were mostly of other kids, boys about two or three. Some of the pictures were of me in my bed with these boys. We were naked under a pink canopy on pink fluffy blankets with our arms around each other. I didn't remember any of it. It was like seeing another version of yourself doing something wrong without you being aware of it.

"Miss Rose, as you got older, did you ever mention your father's activities to your mother? Yes or no?"

"No."

"And why was that?"

"I hardly ever saw my mother. She isn't easy to talk to. My father asked me not to tell her, he said it was something special between us and he was planning to surprise her with beautiful pictures someday."

When court ended for the day, Camille and I took a cab back to the hotel. I was so exhausted, I could barely stand up. Gypsy was raring to go. She wanted to see San Francisco but she wasn't going to see it with me. I laid down on the bed and fell into a deep sleep until Grand woke me at 7 a.m. the next morning. There wasn't enough time now to get my birth certificate; court started at 9 a.m. today. It would have to wait. I didn't expect to feel so tired. I felt like someone drained my insides out. I gave all of me over to court yesterday. Maybe this was what I needed to rid myself of it all. No one knew the whole truth yet, not even Dr. G. My father knew, but he probably thought they didn't have that last picture. He probably thought I'd be too ashamed to talk about it. If he thought that, he was right. I wished I'd heard the testimony of the other witnesses. I didn't know who they were. I imagined Miss Melnyk being called. She didn't know anything, but maybe she did. I couldn't know for sure. Maybe everyone knew except for me. I didn't remember any of those kids in the photographs.

Chapter Five

For another week, eight hours a day, with only an hour off for lunch, I looked at pictures and answered questions.

"Miss Rose." I felt myself cringe when I heard my name. I looked up and saw Miss Cooper at the lectern. I didn't remember going up on the witness stand. "Are you alright?"

"Yes, I'm fine." I wasn't fine, never really had been fine. I needed to look up the word *fine* to see what it truly meant.

"Would you like a minute?" Judge Silverman looked down at me from her heavenly perch. She did seem God-like.

"Permission to approach the witness."

"You may."

"Permission to put Government Exhibit number 1000 on the screen; it's already in evidence, Your Honor."

The Judge gave permission and Miss Cooper proceeded. She directed me to look at the computer screen in front of me. It was a picture of the woman who was walking with my father in the city last summer.

"Do you recognize the woman in this photograph?'

"Yes."

"Do you know her?"

"No."

"Tell the jury where you recognize her from." I turned toward the jury and told them about the day, when I was walking in the city and I saw my father with the woman and the little girl.

"Did your father approach you that day on the street?"

"Yes, he tried to kidnap me." When I said the word, *kidnap*, my father's attorney jumped up from his seat to object. "Your Honor, my client could hardly kidnap his own child. Miss Rose is prejudicing the jury."

"That's debatable, Mr. Mulkey." The Judge turned toward me. "Miss Rose, describe in your own words what happened that day. Just explain the scene and try not to use prejudicial words like *kidnap,* do you understand?" I nodded.

"My father tried to pull me into his car where the woman was waiting. I could see the shadow of the little girl in the backseat. I was in front of my grandmother's apartment building. The doorman saw and saved me."

"Please continue, what happened next?"

"My father left when the doorman came over."

"Did your father speak to you?"

"Yes, he said, I wasn't eighteen yet, and I still belonged to him, that I'd be sorry."

"Did he say anything else?"

"Yes, he said the police came to his apartment. He asked me what I'd told my grandmother about him and that his photography is art, nothing else. He seemed scared."

"Objection, Your Honor, speculation."

"Sustained, the jury will disregard the witness' statement regarding the emotional state of the defendant." Mr. Mulkey returned to his seat with a cocky grin. Miss Cooper continued unfazed.

"Permission to approach the witness with Government Exhibit number 1002, Your Honor?"

"Yes, Miss Cooper." Miss Cooper came close to me, leaned on the ledge of the witness stand and held a photograph out for me.

"Do you recognize the girl in this photograph? Yes or no."

"Yes."

"Where do you recognize her from?

"She's the girl who was with my father and the woman last summer."

The questioning was tedious with no end in sight. The jury appeared restless and a few of them were nodding off. I knew there was a photograph missing from the evidence; I hoped they'd never find it.

Chapter Six

It was Monday morning, the beginning of my third week on the stand and I was still not used to it. I slept most of the weekend, but still had dark circles under my eyes. It was not a good look considering I had dark, almost black eyes and black hair.

"Good morning, Miss Rose, I remind you, you are still under oath."

"Yes, Your Honor, I know."

"Your Honor, may I inquire?" Miss Cooper remained standing at the prosecution table until the Judge consented, then she walked across the back of the other prosecutors and up to the lectern. I wondered how she didn't wear herself out walking like she was knee deep in water.

"Good morning, Miss Rose." They were all so fixated on wishing me a *good morning,* it wasn't a good morning, but I played along and wished her one too.

"Permission to put Government Exhibit number 75 up, but not for the jury, Your Honor? It's not in evidence."

"Do I have a copy here?" The legal staff fumbled through the photographs to see if there was a copy for the Judge; there wasn't. Judge Silverman peered up over her glasses. "Side bar," she said, then she told the jury to *take a moment and stretch.* I put on my *what about me, face,* but got up anyway when no one was looking. I was not the one on trial here. I looked over at the spectators. I noticed a discolored space on the back of the wall where a clock obviously used to be. Wires were hanging in the breeze like the clock had been carved out. I'd been here for all this time and I just noticed it now.

Grand smiled over at me, Camille did the same; Gypsy gave me a *thumbs up*! I looked back up at the clock-less wall and wondered why it had been carved out. What I was really wondering was what was going on at the *side bar*. The lawyers and their teams huddled together while the Judge stood imposingly over them. They looked like they were discussing football strategy, getting ready to call a big play. I daydreamed it was a year from now; where would I be? Would I be over all this? Recovered? Having a new normal life? I hoped so; I deserved to be recovered.

The lawyers left the side of the Judge's perch and returned to their places. Judge Silverman held up her robe, climbed up to her seat, waited for the lawyers to be seated, looked up over the top of her glasses and said, "Miss Cooper, please continue."

"Permission to put Government Exhibit number 75 up for the witness and the attorneys but not the jury, Your Honor?"

The Judge allowed it and I looked up at the photograph on my computer screen. I felt sick, like I was going to throw up here, in front of everyone. I poured water from the pitcher in front of me and took a gulp. I held the paper cup in two hands; I was shaking.

"Miss Rose, do you recognize this photograph? Yes or no?"

"Yes, but please, Miss Cooper, don't make me talk about this. Please!" I felt my eyes well up.

"Permission to approach the witness, Your Honor?"

The Judge granted permission and Miss Cooper walked over to me looking like she wanted to hug me. It wouldn't be a lawyerly thing to do. I looked down in my lap.

"I know this is difficult, Miss Rose, but this is an important piece of evidence, try to be brave."

Brave? It was easy for her to stand there and tell me, *I needed to be brave,* I was brave, had been brave all along. She had no clue. I just didn't want to talk about this. I hated having to admit my father controlled me like this. I hated I had been submissive and fearful. I spent most of my life trapped and tethered to a web spun by my own father. I'd fallen for his idealistic view of himself as a *misunderstood artist*, *ahead of his time.* He was nothing but a fraud. He hurt other people not just me.

He had to be stopped. I'd come this far. I never dreamed my escape to New York would lead to this, but here I was, it would never end if I didn't speak up.

"Miss Rose, once again, do you recognize this photograph? Yes or no?"

"Yes, but Miss Cooper, will you please just call me Jenna?"

Miss Cooper glanced at the Judge who nodded in approval. "Yes of course, if that's what you'd prefer."

"It is, thank you."

"Who is the person in this picture?"

"It's me."

"How do you know that?" she asked as if she already knew the answer.

"I remember it being taken."

"Who took this picture?"

"My father, Alan Rose."

"Permission to publish Government Exhibit number 75 for the jury, Your Honor?"

I heard short gasps coming from the jury box; I kept my head down.

"Your Honor, permission to publish Government Exhibit numbers 76-82 as part of this evidence."

"Jenna, tell the jury the circumstances surrounding this particular photo shoot, in your own words, please."

I felt the lights of interrogation getting brighter. I was exposed; people died of exposure. I remembered reading about hikers in Colorado dying of "exposure." I knew this wasn't the same but I felt like I could die right here on the witness stand. I wanted to swallow myself up whole. I looked over at Grand and thought about her, *living in the now,* mantra. I had no choice, I was trapped, again. I was back there now in the powder puff pink room; I'd never get out of there in my head if I didn't talk about this. I felt like I was watching it all on an old newsreel. It was out there in front of me in vivid detail. I began: "When I woke up on the morning of my thirteenth birthday, I still felt tired. I had a heavy feeling in my stomach and I didn't want to get up. I turned on my side and tried to go back to sleep but I couldn't. I got up slowly and felt something trickle down my leg. It was blood. I knew what was happening; I'd read about it but I didn't know what to do. My mother wasn't home; my father was the only one there. I had no choice but to tell him, ask him what I should do. *This is great,* he said when I told him, then he asked me if there was any blood on the bed." I stopped to take a sip of water.

"Go on, please, Miss Rose, sorry Jenna."

"I told him, no. I didn't understand why he cared at first. I didn't know what he wanted exactly. Then he told me to get back into the bed and to take off my pajamas. I was scared but more afraid to refuse him. So, I did what he said. He left the room but returned a few minutes later with his camera equipment. Then he told me, *Jenna, this is our last photo shoot, the last we will ever have. I need to film this as it's happening to have a proper end, you know, closure.* He explained to me he would no longer be needing my help with his art. He asked me to spread my legs apart but when I hesitated, he leaned forward and did it for me, like he was posing me. Then he brought the camera to his face, hunched lower and started to take shots of the blood as it trickled down my leg, making a red stain on the sheets. I felt really embarrassed and ashamed. And it felt like time was moving in slow motion. He photographed me from every angle. He really got into it. He was acting like he'd just hit the jackpot or something."

"Objection, Judge, the witness is prejudicing the jury again, offering her opinion as to the state of mind of the defendant."

"Not sure about that, Mr. Mulkey, but I will sustain the objection. Jenna, please continue and try to confine your comments to the facts as you remember them."

"Okay."

"Please continue." Miss Cooper was still hovering. I wondered if she had kids, probably not; she seemed to care though. She didn't seem bothered by the stuff she must have seen or heard about day in and day out.

"He asked me to remove the covers from my chest so he could see if *anything was up there.*" The jury was mumbling to each other, shaking their heads, not exactly acting impartial.

"When he finished, I went to take a shower. When I got back to my room, there was a clean set of sheets folded at the foot of the bed with a box of sanitary pads on top."

I felt totally disembodied when I finished telling my story. It felt like it was someone else I was talking about. I looked up at Miss Cooper; I couldn't look at Grand or Gypsy or the strangers on the jury. I felt the enormous weight of humiliation on top of me. I glanced quickly at my father, who had no expression. He just sat there in arrogant silence next to the slimy Mr. Mulkey.

"Jenna, are you alright?"

"Yes, I think so."

"Did you ever see those photographs before today?"

"No." I thought I was finished with the questions but they continued to spew forth like hot lava dripping all over me.

"Do you know what your father did with the pictures he took of you? Yes or no?"

"Yes, I think so."

"How do you know?"

"Someone told me about a website called, *Teasing Tots*. She said pictures of me might have been uploaded there, but she wasn't sure." I didn't want to tell her that Dr. G. was my therapist and give the jury the impression that I was a crazy person. Miss Cooper didn't ask me who had told me, which was a surprise.

"Thank you, Jenna. Nothing further, Your Honor."

"Now is a good time to break for the day." Judge Silverman turned to the jury. "Ladies and gentlemen, you are dismissed for the day. Please return at 11 a.m. tomorrow morning. Court will resume later since I have a meeting in the morning. Please don't discuss the case or look anything up on the Internet. Have a nice evening."

"All rise," Miss Myer instructed as the jury left the courtroom.

The Judge turned toward me. "Are you sure you're okay?" I nodded mechanically.

Don't these people understand that I didn't know what it meant to feel okay or fine or normal? What would she do if I said, *no as a matter of fact, I'm not alright?* Would she leave me alone, excuse me from testifying further? No, she wouldn't, so what was the point of asking? I had told enough truth, now I was lying under oath. I was not alright!

"Okay then, Jenna, please be here by 11 a.m. tomorrow; you're still giving testimony."

She stood from her lofty perch and left through the heavy brass door where the powerful members of the court gathered inside the inner chambers of justice. I wished I had some kind of chamber to hide in.

Chapter Seven

Gypsy was up early; the sun had barely risen and she was dressed and out the door with Gracie. I got up as soon as she left. The smell of room service was trickling under the door from Grand's room. I went in search of coffee; it was 6 a.m. Grand was sitting on the sofa drinking tea. She wasn't a breakfast eater but insisted I eat something. "Have something, Jenna, it's going to be a long day," she said when she heard me come in. She didn't look in my direction. "Have some protein, at least. Where's Gabrielle?"

"Out with Gracie." Grand didn't even mention yesterday's court session. Grand seemed to instinctively know when to keep quiet.

"I wish that kid would let someone know where she's off to." Grand shook her head. I took my coffee and returned to my own room. Gypsy was used to being on her own and not checking in. I lay back on the bed and fell asleep. It was 8:30 when I awoke again. I ran to the shower. I had enough time before court started to go and get my birth certificate. I dressed quickly and left—Gypsy style—without telling anyone. Grand would have to accept it.

The building that held all the records for the northern district of California was across the street from the courthouse. After I got through security, I took a number and waited to be called along with the other thirty or so people who were ahead of me. It was 10:10 by the time my name was called. The woman behind the cubicle took down my information. She never looked up, not once. She had thin, wispy, brownish blonde hair that sat on the top of her head like it had landed there on a windy day, and hadn't moved since.

"Can't find a Jenna Rose born that year in December," she said finally raising her eyes to look at me.

My face dropped down to my chest. She mustered up some sympathy for me and asked if I had anything else which could *facilitate the search.* I showed her my social security number, I had it written down. Then I handed her my passport.

"Nope, sorry, no Jenna Rose. What's your mother's maiden name, honey, and her date of birth? Do you know?" I told her and a second later, she looked up smiling. "Here it is, just a minute and I'll have it for you."

I glanced at the clock; it was intact unlike the clock on the back of the courtroom wall. It said 10:44; by 10:50, I had the envelope I assumed held my birth certificate and I made my way across to the courthouse. I had to run; the defense attorney didn't need ammunition against me. It was his turn now to cross-examine me. I hoped the worst of it would be over soon. All my dirty secrets had been laid out for all those strangers' to hear. I found a kindhearted looking security guard and told him, "I'm a witness for Judge Silverman; I'm almost late. I'm on the stand."

He didn't even answer, he just shouted, "Sitting witness, let her through, c'mon clear a path," I ran through, exchanged my phone for the gold coin and entered the courtroom.

"Please come forward, Jenna." Judge Silverman backward waved me toward her.

Grand turned around gesturing with her hands and mouthed, "Where were you?" I shrugged and held up the manila envelope. I knew she'd figure it out.

"Good morning, Jenna, may I remind you, you are still under oath. Mr. Mulkey, you may inquire."

"Thank you, Judge." Andy, not Andrew Mulkey was wearing a brown suit. It was too big at the shoulders and was too tight in the pants. He had a five o'clock shadow; Grand had mentioned this term to me when Mr. Stanton showed up for a meeting with an unshaven face. Mr. Stanton, I didn't even want to think about him; how he was my stepfather.

I had no experience with court etiquette but even I knew Mr. Mulkey was a bad choice. What was my father thinking? Maybe he was trying to gain the sympathy of the jury by showing he didn't have the money to hire better counsel.

When Mr. Mulkey stood up, the cuff of one of his pant legs caught on to the table tripping him. Legal papers fell to the floor. His assistant, an equally gruff looking younger man, ran to the front of the table to help retrieve them. It was embarrassing. I remembered Grand saying once, *first impressions are lasting impressions,* this, I thought was what the jury would remember. Then he opened his mouth to speak. He wasn't a bad looking man. He had dark brown hair and blue eyes and kind of looked like a slobby George Clooney. But the Clooney resemblance was completely wasted on him. When he spoke, I wondered if he went to law school at all.

"So, Miss Rose." He paused for effect and his fiendishly raspy voice was held in mid-air. A vein in his head was protruding, it was distracting. I looked at the jury to see their reaction. Some were rolling their eyes while looking over at their fellow jurors who were whispering to each other. "Do you know what a ranch house is?"

"A house on farm property, I guess."

"No, Miss Rose, a ranch house is a house that is all on one level, no second story. Would you call your lake home in California where you lived with my client a ranch home or a two-story home?"

"A ranch home, I guess."

"Was there an additional level on the house, anywhere?"

"No, I don't think so."

"Then how is it possible that you were locked in what you referred to as a *dark red room in the attic?"* I didn't answer; I didn't know what to say. My face was flushed.

"Okay, let's talk about something else.

"I hear you like to read. In fact, you are well read for your age. Isn't that true?"

"Yes."

"And you read a lot, you read some pretty impressive works, right?"

"Yes, I guess so."

"Tell me if you recognize this passage:

…the red room was a spare chamber, very seldom slept in…A bed supported on massive pillars of mahogany, hung with curtains of deep red damask…the carpet was red…Daylight began to forsake the red-room…but then prepared as my mind was for horror…I was oppressed, suffocated…

"Do you recognize this passage, Miss Rose?"

"Yes."

"From what book do you recognize it?"

"It's a line from the novel, *Jane Eyre,* by Charlotte Bronte."

"Very impressive, Miss Rose."

"Objection, Your Honor." Suddenly Miss Cooper was out of her chair and on her feet. "I don't see the relevance of this line of questioning."

"I ask for the court's patience, Judge. I'm getting there."

"Please try to get where you're going sometime soon, Mr. Mulkey," Judge Silverman responded.

"Yes, Judge."

"Once again, Miss Rose, is there an attic in the lake house on Sulphur Mine Road where you lived with your parents?"

"No, I guess not." I was starting to sweat; my face was hot and flushed. I could feel my pulse pounding in my neck and I felt hot and cold at the same time.

"Is it possible, Miss Rose, you are confusing the scene in the book, *Jane Eyre*, with actual events from your own life?"

"Maybe, I'm not sure, no I don't think so."

"Did your father, the defendant, ever lock you in an attic room?"

"No, I guess not, maybe it was somewhere else."

"Are you just making things up, Miss Rose?"

"Objection, Your Honor, badgering the witness." I was crying now. I may have imagined the attic or possibly dreamt it. I was so confused now but even though everything else happened like I said it did, they wouldn't believe me now."

"Over-ruled, Mr. Mulkey, please watch your tone and your line of questioning."

Ignoring the Judge's instruction, Mr. Mulkey continued, "One more thing for today, Miss Rose; are you a virgin?"

"Objection, Your Honor," Miss Cooper shouted as the jurors' gasped in sync. "The witness isn't on trial here." The Judge frowned; it was obvious she was not a fan of Mr. Mulkey's.

"Speaks to credibility, Judge."

"Sidebar, Your Honor," Miss Cooper requested. She swooped up some papers and headed to the side of the courtroom, opposite the jurors. The other attorneys stood along with the court stenographer who carried her steno machine over to the side of the Judge's desk. I could hear arguing, but not the words they were saying. I thought the worst was behind me; I didn't expect this. How could I think there was an attic in the lake house? It felt so real. It happened somewhere if only I could remember. Now, I had to answer that vile question. What could I say? The question would require a yes or no response, but it wasn't that simple. My father invaded my privacy for as long as I could remember. He crept into my being with his "art." He didn't rape me in the physical sense; he raped my childhood, robbed me of a normal child's life. He tried to take my soul, my essence. I only knew what I was missing when I started to read about other people and how they lived. Of course, I was a virgin, but I'd still been violated. I didn't know how I was going to answer. Gypsy would think I was a freak if she didn't already. I was probably the only eighteen-year old virgin left on the planet. I was a freak.

The lawyers returned to their respective positions. "Mr. Mulkey, you may continue but watch your line of questioning."

"Yes, Judge, I'll withdraw the question." I felt relief wash over me but then he asked, "So, Miss Rose, did you enjoy being your father's *Lolita*? You are familiar with that book, aren't you?"

"Objection, Your Honor, please! Mr. Mulkey is attempting to put the witness on trial."

Miss Cooper shouted and her face turned red.

"Perhaps, Miss Cooper is unfamiliar with young girls these days and how… enticing they can be." With that, Miss Cooper requested another sidebar. Once again, the lawyers, their assistants, the stenographer and the Judge huddled at the corner of the Judge's perch.

Fifteen minutes later, they were still huddled around the judge. I looked in my lap at the manila envelope. May as well have a look at my birth certificate. Here it was, my beginnings in black and white: Baby girl born to Meghan O'Connor, my date of birth was written underneath, below that. Father: Unknown. Father Unknown—What?

Emily Dickinson's poem, *I'm nobody, are you nobody too?* rang in my ears repeatedly along with Grand's words, *you have a story now.* My story was morphing into an epic. I was shaking. This was another bombshell moment. The fallout from this blast had landed on me. I looked over at my father, at Alan. Who was he? Did my mother think I would never find this out? Did Grand know? My life was a cosmic joke. I felt myself deconstructing. I was unhinging, floating in space untethered now by any anchor. But was I ever anchored, really? I looked over at Grand and Gypsy. Could they be trusted? Could anyone? Were they really on my side? I imagined the fantastical. Were they all part of some sinister ring? I wondered if a person could become dead rather than just outright die. It seemed I had; I had no identity; I fell off the wall and what never existed couldn't be put back together again. My mind was racing. This sudden shock, this bolt, I imagined was how Cleopatra must have felt when the asp bit her. Life was about to change, again.

I heard muffled voices, like people were talking underwater. My ears were fuzzy, full of cotton. Mr. Mulkey was back. The Judge was saying something; I didn't know what. I was a *Trompe l'oeil* girl. I was never real. I was a *fool the eye*, fool the world, even fool the girl herself creation.

"Miss Rose," Mr. Mulkey called over to me. I looked at him hard, lowering my eyebrows, confused.

"Judge," Mr. Mulkey said throwing up his arms.

"Jenna, do you need a moment?"

I looked up at her and held my birth certificate in my hand, reaching out toward her. Everything was blurry, like I was in a dream or maybe drunk. Miss Myer appeared, took the birth certificate and handed it to the Judge. She studied it for a minute, placed it on her desk and announced, "Court is adjourned for the day. We will resume tomorrow afternoon. Jenna, you may be excused for the day in light of this new information." She gave her usual instructions to the jury.

"Your Honor," both attorneys yelled at the same time.

"Court is adjourned until noon tomorrow. I will see the attorneys in my chambers." She turned toward me holding up the envelope with my birth certificate in it. "Jenna, may I keep this for the time being?" I nodded my head, far too shook up to speak.

"All rise," Miss Myer shouted.

The jurors filed out in a line with perplexed expressions. Judge Silverman stepped down and the attorneys followed behind her and beyond the brass door and into the inner chamber. I felt small, like I'd fallen down the rabbit hole and into an alternate universe. I held onto the wooden railing and stepped down off the witness stand.

Chapter Eight

No one spoke on the car ride back. All the "Gs" were piled in the back seat. Camille stayed behind to join the other lawyers in the Judge's chambers. I sat in the front with the driver. I was walking through a dream. It was like my whole body had missing parts; I had phantom body syndrome. I didn't feel real. My life, while not wonderful, had been mine. Now, just when I thought it was getting better, just when I started having hope that at least I was safe, this happened. Now I had no self, no truth.

The car pulled into the driveway of the hotel. Grand excused the driver for the day and everyone stood on the curb in silence looking at me, waiting for me to say something, to fill them in on the latest episode. Before the questions started, I said, "I'm going for a walk, I'll see you later." I took Gracie's leash from Gypsy and headed across the street to the bay.

Grand gave me two hours before she sent Gypsy to look for me. Gypsy made a pit stop at the glass-covered mall between the hotel and the bay. I turned when I heard her call out, "Thinking of jumping?" I moved away from the railing and smiled when I saw her carrying six shopping bags, three on each arm.

"No, but I was dealt a bad hand, don't you think?"

"So, go fish," she said without a moment's hesitation, her copper eyes flashing. I assumed she was referring to the kid's card game. "You know, when you don't like the cards you have, you throw them back and pick another set."

"Very funny." She had a point; I was at a crossroads again anyway. I could wallow—as Grand would say—or move on. This was the perfect time to reinvent myself. I had no real identity anyway. I could be whomever I chose to be. I might not even be related to Alan J. Rose. This would be great news, a gift from the gods. But as much as I hated him right now, I hated my mother more.

Gypsy didn't give me a chance to say anything else. Instead she told me I was feeling sorry for myself. She told me how she had spent most of her childhood with nannies and then all alone when she outgrew the need for one. Now she had me and soon she would have a husband.

"You know what Adele would say to me when I acted up? Which, by the way, I did a lot so I could get her attention."

"No, what?"

"You are a few crusts short of a loaf. Nice, huh? She thought that was so hysterical. It might have been if she ever told me anything else."

"Yeah, well, *quirky* was what Alan called me. He said it when he first noticed me picking the chipped paint from the wainscoting on my bedroom wall. I was on the bed waiting for the day's photo session to end. It was cold. *Hang on now, Jenna, just a few more pictures and we'll be done for now.* It's what he'd always say and then it would go on for hours more until he would get it right. Picking at the peeling paint made me feel like I was in control of something. A little scratch on the paint and down it would fall in pieces behind the bed and onto the pink carpet in that sickly pink room, which Alan had decorated just for me. It really had been for him. It was just a stage, a set where his 'art' could be created."

I paused. Should I tell her about the birth certificate? No, instead I said, "then he left without a word of goodbye. There wasn't even a fight. He and Meghan never fought, they rarely spoke. It's all making sense now, the whole thing. They never even came close to each other."

"What makes sense now, Jenna?" I didn't answer, I just continued with my rant.

"For as long as I can remember, Alan held me in his realm of monstrous self-delusions vacillating between grandeur and persecution. I read this someplace and it seems to fit him. One minute, I was his pride and joy and the next I was a curse he was saddled with. All makes sense now.

You are my main girl, couldn't be what I am without you. We belong together, like two peas in a pod, he would say, while adjusting his camera. His hairy hands would stick out from under his starched pink shirt. Then a minute later, he would scream, *what the hell is wrong with you? Bend your knees when I tell you to and take that blanket off.* It was on the last day when he told me, *I need someone younger now;* I had just turned thirteen. But I was there every day before then, as long as he wanted me, as long as he needed me to create his twisted empire. I never knew what he did with those pictures; I never asked. I was alone then, I always dreamed about having a real family, like the ones in the books I read, maybe have a horde of sisters like Jo and Amy in *Little Women.* Maybe this is why I confused *Jane Eyre*, with my own life. It seemed the same to me; trauma is trauma, no matter what the color is in the room where it is happening."

It felt good to say all this to Gypsy. But what I was really doing was spewing it into the universe and off of my shoulders. I was surprised when I looked up and saw her copper eyes were full of tears.

"Now, you do have a family, Jenna. So, you should try to count the good stuff. Dump all those crappy memories in the bay before you go back to your new home, your real home. Do it when this part is finally over. Life changes all the time. These feelings won't last forever."

"How old are you?" I asked laughing.

Chapter Nine

It wasn't easy to dump it all. When we returned to the hotel, Grand had room service waiting. Camille still wasn't back from court. The four of us ate in silence. Dr. G seemed to be watching me closely for signs of hysteria, I guess. I knew they were waiting for me to tell them what happened, what it was that delayed the court proceedings. I wasn't ready to.

"Excuse me, I'm going to bed now."

It was more like a coma than a night's sleep. The clock radio on the side of the nightstand clearly stated 12 p.m. It must be wrong. If it wasn't, I missed court. Why didn't someone wake me? I jumped out of bed and swung open the door to Grand's side. She, along with Dr. G and Camille were sitting at the dining room table looking like they were having a conference. They stopped talking when they saw me; I felt spooked. It reminded me of the scene in *Rosemary's Baby* when Mia Farrow walked into Ruth Gordan's apartment and all the devil worshippers turned to look at her. Gypsy wasn't here. She must be out with Gracie.

"Who died?" I said, trying to deflect my obvious fear.

"No one, your father pled out." Camille stood and moved toward me. We sat side by side on the couch.

"What does that mean? Oh, and I don't think he's my father."

"I know, I haven't told anyone."

"What are you talking about?" Grand asked. She came over to join us. I told her the whole sordid story of my discovery in court. She sat in stunned silence. I felt less afraid but asked her, "did you know about this?"

"No, Jenna, of course not. I just assumed he was. I had no reason to think otherwise. I didn't even know you existed until you were over a year old. Your mother was perpetually mad at us, your grandfather and me, for reasons that escaped us. It was probably some perceived injustice only she was privy to. I intend to get to the bottom of this, for your sake." She was whispering, and seemed distraught. I didn't want anything to happen to her. This was all too much.

"It's okay, I just want to move on, forget it."

I didn't really. I would like to know who I was and where I came from, but I didn't want to make my grandmother ill. The stress of this whole thing was taking a toll on her. I turned to Camille. "Can we go back to New York now?"

"The Judge may want to meet with you before she passes sentence on Mr. Rose, but I'm not sure. I'll know more later on today. Jenna, I need to tell you something."

"What now?"

"Your mother was recalled this morning. She'll probably be charged."

"What about Alan's girlfriend?"

"She pled out as well. She testified against him. I guess it's okay to tell you she's guilty of kidnapping as well as aiding and abetting. She allegedly took her niece out of state without parental consent. She may get a lesser sentence but not by much. Her sister isn't interested in dropping the charges. She put her niece in harm's way. This Judge is no-nonsense. This has been an on-going case. Investigations have been underway for a few years, it just took time to gather witnesses and to get them to come forward. It wasn't easy. There were quite a few of them. Your fath…I mean Mr. Rose will go away for a while."

"Who were the witnesses?"

"I'm not at liberty to say for now. I can't discuss the whole case until after the sentencing. After that time, I will have access to the court records and then I'll be able to convey the testimony of every witness if you want to hear it."

"I'm not sure I want to know but why did he plead out all of a sudden, just like that? He seemed so cavalier during the trial, defensive and self-righteous, at least on the surface."

"He thought he had a sweet defense, immortalizing his beautiful daughter, but the possibility you aren't his blew up in his face. He may or may not know what the truth is. My sense is he knows. And of course, Meghan knows the truth. Mr. Rose is an opportunistic predator who stalked vulnerable women and children. You know, Jenna, it's likely you'll be eligible for a cash settlement."

I felt anger rising up my neck. "Hand me some cash after this is over, seriously, is that supposed to make this better? Put a cash Band-Aid on the wounds and I should do what with it? Get stuff to ease my pain, or set up a perv memorial?"

"Calm down, Jenna, you could put the money to good use. Best not to wallow now." Grand patted my arm like I was a dog. It occurred to me now, Grand was still suffering from the residual effects of Aunt Eileen's syndrome of not showing your feelings: *One needs to bury their emotions, don't wear them on your sleeve and never air your dirty laundry in public.* But I wasn't in public, I was in hell and supposedly with people who cared.

"Listen to me, everyone, I've no name, no identity, no father and currently not much of a mother. As bad as my history was, at least it had been something. Now what do I do? I could have a father somewhere, siblings, even aunts and uncles and maybe another grandmother, who knows? I may never know. What kind of mother does this?" My head was starting to hurt. I couldn't even cry.

"I don't know, Jenna, I just don't. I'm not making excuses for Meghan, but she must have felt desperate to be duped by Alan Rose. She was too stubborn to come home to me. It's just awful, I know but you have me now and nothing is going to change that. Not ever, do you understand?" Grand appeared to be crying but no tears were falling.

Chapter Ten

I sat around the hotel thinking about my state of non-existence for two straight days before being notified it would take another day or so before Judge Silverman would have time to see me. The weather was spring-like despite the time of year. Summer eluded San Francisco. The air was sweet smelling and if the city were people-free, it could release me to feel happy. But as Hemingway said, "*The only thing that could spoil a day was people,* he called them, *Always the limiters of happiness, except for a few.*" He had a point, but it seemed he had to qualify his remarks by adding that last line. I had no desire to do that; I was wary of everyone.

Pushing through the crowds on Market Street with no real destination in mind was unappealing. Luxury hotels were mixed in with low-end stores. Beggars mingled with tourists and shoppers. The homeless resided on one side of the wide street. The year-round mild weather must make a life on the street easier than in the freezing Northeast. But judging by the cool summer weather I wondered about that. Food was another issue; they, like their New York counterparts carried their worldly goods in shopping carts. They were all different ages and sizes. Along with a few homeless families, they sat on the downtown side of the street in a wide corridor as if they were waiting for a rebirth of some kind. I knew the feeling, sort of. But I had help, maybe that was what they were waiting for. I felt better being outside, less alone and suddenly maybe just a little more prepared for what's coming next. But still, I needed time to *wallow* and Grand would have to let me do so. It would take as long as it would take. I see the Judge in two days, and I wondered what she wanted. Maybe she was going to tell me Alan was getting the electric chair and I'd get to pull the switch.

I was really afraid she was going to tell me I screwed up with my false memory and Alan was getting off and would be totally free to wreak havoc with my life and maybe some other girl's. I felt like a prisoner. I just wanted to return to New York and leave all of this behind me here in San Francisco.

Chapter Eleven

The Judge's chamber was located behind two heavy brass doors. I felt like I was being summoned to the principal's office or a meet and greet with St. Peter. Miss Myer met me in the lobby and swiped her ID card in front of the electric eye on the side of the mahogany desk to gain access to the inner chamber. Judge Silverman was alone. She stood when I came in and walked around her desk to greet me. I'd only seen her up on her perch in court. She was less imposing in this setting and surprisingly short. She removed her robe and gestured for me to take a seat. She sat next to me.

"First, I want to return this to you." She handed me the envelope containing my birth certificate. "I can only imagine how you must be feeling, Jenna." She looked at me with her eyes lowered as if she had been the one who'd done something wrong. She was shaking her head.

I didn't respond. I didn't know how I felt. There were so many issues: my mother remarried and pregnant and Alan probably not being my real father; my mother leaving me with a possible stranger all those years, not knowing who my real father was and if I had siblings or other grandparents, but most of all not knowing who I really was. I wanted to be anyone else right now and anywhere else but here. For a fleeting moment, I thought about Jude and wondered if he would have taken care of me like he said he would. Who knew if he could have been trusted either? He could have been the Alan of the drug scene and I could have ended up camped out with the bunch on the Market Street corridor. I couldn't think about him. I had been the one who called the cops. I had been the one who had been a betrayer if you thought about it, but I was not going to think about it, not now, not ever. Maybe my mother was just too weak to resist the lure of Alan and his lies. At least I was stronger than she was.

The Judge was staring at me and snapped me to this surreal reality. "Jenna… Jenna, are you okay? Would you like some water?" I shook my head.

"I want you to know there's no record of Mr. Rose adopting you or stepping forward to claim you as his child. Your name isn't legally Jenna Rose. You can change it to whatever name you want. O'Connor, perhaps, since that was your mother's name at the time of your birth. I can help you do that. You should talk to your mother about the personal aspects and dynamics of your family situation. I'm not the one to talk to you about it. I want to talk to you about the sentencing."

Talk to my mother, why would she tell me anything now? This was a huge convoluted web of lies and deceit. I sat quietly trying hard not to scream.

"It will be a few weeks before I pass sentence on Mr. Rose. You can be present in the court if you wish, this is your right. But it's not necessary unless you want to make a statement. I also wanted to tell you in person, your mother has been charged as an accessory. She pled guilty to endangering the welfare of a child. Considering her personal circumstances and the fact she is cooperating with the court, it's possible her sentence may not be what you'd expect. Mr. Rose, as of now, has not agreed to any of the terms of his plea. He has not come forward with any information regarding any of the other suspects in this case and his sentence will reflect this."

"What do you mean other suspects?"

The Judge pushed her hair back and away from her eyes. Her hair was pulled up on top of her head but the shorter ends kept falling out of the clip. She didn't look crisp and neat like the judges on television. It was obvious there was no makeup artist on the set of this courthouse. She stood, got a few Bobby pins out of her desk drawer and put two of them on either side of her head. It wasn't a good look either and I was glad Gypsy wasn't here to comment. When she returned to my side of the desk, instead of sitting, she stood in front of me and took my hand in hers.

"Jenna, Mr. Rose is a convicted child pornographer. He used the Internet to promote his *art* as he liked to call it. There are others involved, do you understand? This is a ring of felons we must stop. The sites have been shut down for now, and the vermin who feed on them have crawled back into their holes, but they will resurface; they always do. It's our job to stop them. We may need Mr. Rose to come forward and help us to do that. Do you understand?"

"Yes, I understand," I replied, but it seemed to me she was setting the stage for Alan to get off easy.

She looked down at me with an expression of sympathy. "If he agrees to help us, I may reduce his sentence but not necessarily. What he did to you and to other children was despicable and can't be easily dismissed, no matter what the terms. I want you to be aware of all possible outcomes. You don't have to be present at the sentencing. You are free to return to New York. It's your call."

"Thank you, Your Honor." Judge Silverman still had my hand in hers. When I stood up to leave, she took my other hand too. Her pale blue eyes stared intently into mine through the reading glasses which balanced across the lower part of her nose, "I've been a judge for fifteen years and I want you to know you are the bravest witness I've ever heard give testimony. I wish you a wonderful new beginning and a bright future. I know you'll do well. Move on as quickly as you can. Don't let this define you and cause irreparable damage. Try to put it behind you and try hard not to wallow too long in the memory of this time." There was the word *wallow* again.

She released my hands somewhat reluctantly, reached onto the top of her desk, handed me her card and said, "Call me anytime, if you need anything at all."

Miss Myer came in to the chamber to escort me out of the courthouse. I glanced out toward the street and saw Grand and Dr. G leaning against the limo. Gypsy was walking Gracie along the curb. I shrugged my shoulders and let out a sigh when I saw them.

"C'mon, hurry up," Gypsy yelled up at me. "We're all packed; we need get to the airport. Our flight leaves in three hours." I looked over at Grand. "How did you know I would want to leave and not stay for the sentencing?"

"You've been through enough, it's in the hands of the universe now. Besides, I can't have you wallowing around here anymore; we have a wedding coming up. Let's get going."

The limo sped up Market Street toward the Bay Bridge. I peered out across the four-lane road and watched as a trolley car passed by a line of shopping carts. Beside the carts were two men who were facing each other; each man was holding one end of a torn shirt they must have pulled out of the garbage. Their mouths were open and they seemed to be arguing while tugging on the shirt in opposite directions. I turned my head away from the window, face forward and didn't look back. Suddenly, I knew what I wanted: I didn't want to be special or brave or different or damaged. I just wanted to be ordinary.

Chapter Twelve

The apartment renovations continued without us while we were in California. They were finished. Gypsy was the first one to open the door to the newly added rooms.

"Wow! It's Narnia, a whole new land," she said while exploring the new territory. I could hear her *oohing and ahhing,* but I was too tired to care. Grand went into the kitchen first. I poked my head in and saw her opening up the Safe Serve Certificate. "Ha, look at this, after all this time."

"Hmm," was all I had the strength to say to her. I found my way to bed and slept for twenty hours straight. It was mid-afternoon the next day by the time I woke up.

"You slept the sleep of the newly released," Grand announced when I came into the kitchen. I wasn't sure what she meant. I was regenerating, I guess, trying to become who I was supposed to be, restoring myself back to the original, "should have been" me.

Grand turned to answer the phone and I left the kitchen but listened by the door. Old habits took long to die. She was talking to Camille, "Great, you found her, thanks." I lingered a minute and then heard Grand hang up and dial another number. Without missing a beat or even saying hello, she said, "You have an obligation to your daughter, you owe her a history, an explanation, something…"

Meghan must have hung up because the conversation ended. I didn't want my mother's explanations. Imagining her excuses were preferable to any made-up excuses she would give me. I took coffee to my room, found my journal and sat down to write. I'd forgotten to bring it with me to California; my last entry was well over a month ago. I opened to a blank page and wrote:

My mother died today. She didn't know who I was at the end; she didn't know who I was at the beginning. She never saw me. I was transparent, I wasn't there.

I know it's not proper to disrespect the dead, but she's not really dead, she's only dead to me.

I tried hard to cut Meghan some slack, to muster up some sympathy for what may have gone on in her life to make her do what she did, to make the choices she made, but in the end, I just couldn't feel sorry for her. I wasn't going to feel sorry for myself either. I'd done enough of that. Looking back and rehashing it all over and over was not going to happen, moving forward was. There was no way I was going to be a victim.

PART FOUR

Chapter One

Gypsy listed me as J. O'Connor in her wedding brochure or whatever you call it. I hadn't exactly changed my name yet, but Gypsy started calling me "J" and it stuck, with her anyway. She thought Jenna was a contrived name, a good name for a kitten. Considering, she went by the name Gypsy, I didn't take her too seriously.

Judge Silverman had offered to help me out with the legal process of a name change. For now, I was still a nobody. I was not sure I even wanted to change my first name—kitten-like or not, it was all I had of me. The rest of me was erased, now I had to create a new "myself," a replacement me. I thought I was coping fairly well, considering I sent Alan to prison and my mother was out on a hefty bail.

Alan, according to Camille, Grand's hot shot attorney, was kicking around the idea of submitting what they called a "5K" letter to the court. In exchange for testifying against the bigger fish that set up all those websites, he would get a lesser sentence or be out entirely. No promises, according to the prosecutor. He could rot in prison for all I cared. He was such a coward; I doubted he had the nerve to rat anyone out. When I'd first arrived in court, he sat there so smug, like he expected a convent full of nuns to attest to the fact he was innocent. He expected the meek little girl he used and abused to take the stand, instead he got an empowered New York City woman testifying against him. Surprise, asshole!

Chapter Two

James insisted his friend Madeline be a bridesmaid. Gypsy wanted only me as maid of honor but caved into James' request. Madeline was full of herself. We had already picked out my dress so a last-minute match had to be created for her. I didn't get this relationship at all. Madeline was cadaver thin and her pale complexion made it easy to imagine her laid out in a coffin in her new navy-blue gown. She was wispy frail and blonder than Alan's translucent girlfriend. Even so, she did look better in navy than I did with my dark eyes and nearly black hair. We were opposite ends of the spectrum. Gypsy, however, looked stunning in her wedding dress. It was lace with hints of sparkle hidden here and there. No one would be looking at me or Madeline.

The wedding was done up to perfection. Adele, who didn't show up for graduation, was there to lord over the festivities. She barely gave Gypsy any attention. The ceremony was generic but tasteful. Gypsy's father, whom she rarely ever mentioned, not only showed up to walk her down the aisle but he also paid for the entire wedding, including my dress. He was attentive to both Gypsy and me. He seemed to know all about me. It left me wondering if Gypsy's relationship with him was less stormy than she'd claimed.

Gypsy seemed lost at her own wedding reception. James was standing at the bar with a group of guys, and Madeline was hanging on his arm looking bridal. Watching this from my seat was enough to make me vomit. Maybe it was none of my business, but I didn't think Gypsy thought this through.

"Hey, J, do you want to get out of here? Let's go visit my grandmother, show her my dress."

Gypsy enlisted one of the limo drivers and we headed to the Bronx. She presented herself, once again, at the gravesite of Ella F. Booker, her maternal grandmother. Gypsy posed and spun around to give the dead woman a full view of her dress, like she expected her to fawn over her. I couldn't take it.

"Gypsy, what are we doing here? Why aren't you at your own wedding? If you wanted to visit your grandmother, why am I here with you and not James?"

"He'd think it was weird."

"He'd have to get in line. Why did you marry him anyway? He seems so—I don't know—disinterested." At first, she didn't answer, but then she whispered something I couldn't hear.

"What?"

"I'm pregnant."

"Gypsy, if he isn't interested in you, what makes you think he'll be interested in a baby?"

"No, he loves me, he's just distracted." Yeah, by Madeline, I thought but didn't say.

"C'mon, let's get back, you don't want to miss out on your own wedding day."

Adele appeared frantic when she saw us.

"Here we go," Gypsy said as Adele began her tirade, "just where the hell have the two of you been? Don't you know there are important clients of mine here? How does it look to have the bride go missing? Madeline had to step in and do the first dance with James. Serves you right, Gabrielle."

Gypsy stormed into the ballroom, walked forcefully up to Madeline and slapped her hard in the face. Some guests were stunned, most weren't. James had been flaunting his whatever relationship with Madeline, humiliating his bride. He was a shit of monumental proportions and Gypsy didn't deserve this. I looked over at Madeline, she was crying on James' shoulder, milking the situation. Her face was cherry red on one side; the slap seemed to have improved her sallow complexion.

Gypsy was nowhere; no one had any idea where she had gone. The wedding reception went on without the bride and months passed by before I saw her again, and then it wasn't exactly in the flesh.

Chapter Three

I was feeling lonely. It was an odd feeling since I'd been alone for most of my life, but now that I knew what I was missing, loneliness hit hard. I deferred college but would be starting in the spring. Gypsy hadn't spoken to me since our wedding day visit to her grandmother's grave and my own grandmother was busy with her own life. I warded off despair by walking Gracie for at least a mile every day. Passing by a news stand outside the subway station on West 59th Street, I noticed a very pregnant Gypsy on the cover of a magazine.

"Wow! She's a friend of mine," I told the disinterested merchant.

"May I have one of those, please."

"Just one?"

"Okay, two." I figured Grand would want a copy for herself. Maybe, not sure though, because there on the cover was Gypsy, at least six months pregnant wearing a belly shirt with her pregnant self, exposed to the world. I didn't like it. It took a pregnancy to get her a cover shot. She didn't look happy, but most cover girls didn't. I wondered if she was still with James. Adele moved to California, permanently. It seemed to be the haven state for deadbeat moms. Their apartment had been sold.

I didn't have to wonder long whether or not Gypsy was still with James.

"Answer the door, please Jenna." I didn't change my first name, only my last. I'd had enough change. But a new life was starting. I had been accepted to college, had started in January; now I was looking forward to my first spring break. Of course, I'd spend it with Grand but it was still another landmark.

Gypsy's enormous self was at the door. "Can I come in, please? I need to sit down."

"Yes, of course. What are you doing here?"

"I left James, I'm having my bags sent over here, is that okay?"

"Of course, it's okay," I heard Grand say from behind me.

"I'm having twins," Gypsy said, bursting into tears. I'd never seen her cry before.

"It'll be all right, we'll take care of you, all of you, right Grand?" I didn't have a clue how to take care of a pregnant woman-teenager or babies. I hoped Grand knew what we were getting into. She did, as it turned out.

Grand was energized by her new position as Grand Marshall of Gypsy's pregnancy and delivery. I saw spring break fading away. The entire month of March was spent shopping for baby furniture, furnishings, baby clothes times two, stuff and more stuff.

Like a tsunami hit, the new, once empty addition to our apartment filled to capacity, overflowing with baby paraphernalia. Gypsy took one of the bedrooms; she and Grand decorated one of the others for the babies. Gypsy had no interest in knowing the sex of the twins; boys, girls or one of each didn't matter to her. It was exciting. I thought back to two years ago when I was trapped in the lake house; I had no one, not one person whom I could call part of my family with pride. Now, I knew for a fact, you didn't have to be born into a family, a family could arrive and present itself to you and all together you could make it your own. It all happened so fast. What if I'd never left the lake house? What if I'd never met Gypsy? Suddenly, I felt something strange come over me; it was luck. I felt lucky, for once. It was a feeling I'd never felt before.

Chapter Four

Gypsy's water broke the weekend before spring break started. According to Nick, the doorman, in her typical defiant fashion, Gypsy was standing outside in front of the building with an unlit cigarette dangling from her mouth, no doubt trying to get a passerby's attention when a sudden sharp pain and a gush of water derailed her amusement. When no cab would stop, Nick called 911.

Grand and I rushed to the hospital where we found Gypsy writhing in pain. She was easy to locate, we just followed the screams and curses down the hall. It was embarrassing but the nurses seemed unfazed. Gypsy had refused Lamaze classes, *it's just a scam for doctors to charge for something else.* I read up on it and had armed myself with the breathing techniques just in case she needed me. I secretly hope she didn't.

"I'm scared," she whispered to me while the nurses unlocked her bed, getting ready to move her into the delivery room.

"Do you want me to call James?" I stupidly hoped for a romantic bedside reconciliation.

"Hell no!" Gypsy was calmer now after the epidural. "He's in Bermuda with Madeline; I don't want him here as much as he doesn't want to be here."

"He's their father, Gypsy."

"And my father is my father, what's your point? James doesn't care; he thought I was some rich bitch from the Upper West Side who would pull him up from his nobody status to the jet set. He should've married Adele; she loves him. Both of them are shallow, always "vulturing" around, looking for the next best thing. When he found out my father was the one with the money, and he was nowhere near dead, he bolted back into the bony arms of Madeline; will you come with me?"

"Me? How about Grand? She'll know what to do, I…"

She wouldn't let me finish. "C'mon, J, you don't have to do anything, you just have to be there." The nurse handed me a blue gown and I was swept up in the frenzy of labor and delivery.

"Let's move, people," the doctor yelled. "She's ready to push, almost fully dilated, let's go."

Two minutes later, we were in the Delivery Room. Grand gave a half wave and walked in the opposite direction toward the waiting area.

Time seemed to have stood still. In reality, four hours had passed before I made my way to the waiting room to give Grand the news. She was sitting alone in the corner looking old and tired. I sensed worry in her. She looked like she'd aged rapidly in the time it took for Gypsy to give birth. I'd been so busy, caught up in the excitement, so entrenched in the process of helping Gypsy push out the babies, I'd completely forgotten Grand was out here alone, waiting for news. Of course, she was worried. She stood up unsteadily when she saw me approaching.

"Jenna, is everything okay?"

"Yes, she had a hard time, but everyone is fine."

"Everyone?"

"Yes, everyone, now includes two new additions: a boy and a girl born five minutes apart. It was amazing. Their names are Isaiah and Ella Kate. The girl has your name as her middle name, isn't that great?" Grand seemed too exhausted to care.

"Why don't you go home and get some rest? Gypsy's worn out anyway, you can see them all later." It seemed strange for me to be telling Grand what to do. It scared me.

Chapter Five

The shades in Gypsy's room were pulled; she and Isaiah were sleeping quietly but Ella was fussing in her plastic bassinet. I'd never held a baby before, but the urge overwhelmed me. I placed my one hand under her tiny head and my other arm under her body. I lifted her and together we walked over to the chair by the window. I was deep in baby love when the nurse walked in.

"Are you Jenna O'Connor?"

"Yes," I said without looking up. I couldn't seem to take my eyes off of the baby.

"Your grandmother told me you were here. She fainted in the lobby and is downstairs in Emergency."

"Oh my God, is she okay? Will you take Ella? I have to go to her."

The nurse took the baby and I ran off without looking back. *Please let her be okay,* I whispered to myself over and over while pounding the elevator button. It reminded me of the day I escaped from Alan on the street. It was the day I met Gypsy. So much had happened since then; I was not the same person. If something happened to Grand, how would I take care of Gypsy and her babies by myself? I knew I was being selfish for thinking these thoughts when Grand may be sick or dying. But there was no one else.

The clerk at the desk was entering data onto his computer and didn't seem to notice me. I coughed but still no response. "Hello, can you tell me where I can find Katherine O'Connor?"

He pointed to the cubicle on his right without averting his eyes from the computer. I swallowed hard. I thought my lump in the throat days were behind me. I felt my face flushing when I pulled back the curtain. Grand was sitting in a chair on the side of a stretcher. She looked better than she did in the waiting room. Before I had a chance to say anything, the E.R. doctor entered the room.

"Well, what happened to you, young lady?" He was talking to Grand, "Can you hop up on here on the stretcher for a minute so I can examine you? Who's this pretty lady?"

I thought he was being condescending to us both but this wasn't the time for political correctness. At least he didn't call me, "Sweetie." Any other time Grand would have been all over this but she just answered, "My granddaughter, Jenna."

The doctor sent a technician in to draw blood. I didn't know what to do; I needed two Me's—one to be with Gypsy and the other me to stay here with Grand.

"I'm going outside for a minute, Grand, will you be okay?"

"I'm just a little woozy, probably just need to eat something. I'll be fine, don't worry now."

Once outside, I opened my phone. Who should I call? Dr. G? Camille? Camille would be the best, she knew all of Grand's business. She'd know what to do.

Chapter Six

Camille was out of the office; her secretary took the message and promised Camille would get it as soon as she came in. Three hours later, I heard Camille ask the same disinterested clerk where Grand was. I opened the curtain and fell into her arms.

"Grand fainted in the lobby. I left her alone when I was with Gypsy. I should've checked on her, I should've taken her home. The doctor says she had a TIA—a small stroke. What's going to happen now? I'm so scared, Camille."

"None of this is your fault, Jenna. Katherine will be fine. They can treat this. She's going to be okay. Why don't you check on Gypsy. I'll stay here and text you when Katherine wakes up."

Grand had fallen asleep mid-sentence after the nurse finished drawing blood and starting the I.V.

"What did Gypsy have? Boys? Girls?"

"One of each."

Without a moment's hesitation, Camille went into lawyer mode, thank God or whomever, and took charge of Grand's road to recovery. It was the role my mother should have taken. Gypsy's care had fallen to me. It was a role I hoped I could handle. Fortunately, or unfortunately, both Grand and Gypsy were being discharged on the same day. Panic rose up again from my stomach to my throat and back down. I'd better put my acting suit back on. I was beginning to feel like there was an invisible hand pushing me through life.

"Do you think you can drive one of these?" Camille asked while perusing the rental car website. "A Zipcar would be perfect since we only need the car for a day but they're all too small."

"Me? I can't drive; I don't have my license yet."

"Great, me neither."

How a former prosecutor from Long Island survived without a driver's license was a mystery. I gave her a strange look but didn't think it was appropriate to pry. It didn't matter, she told me anyway.

"I used to drive, I don't anymore. I was the prosecuting attorney on so many drunk-driving cases I became phobic about driving. Some of the cases were horrific with the drunk driver walking away unscathed while entire families were wiped out. I just couldn't get back behind the wheel and still have trouble just getting in a car, even as a passenger. I felt like a sitting duck; like I would be the next victim. Weird, right? The odds were in my favor that I would be safe but I felt it wasn't worth the risk. I'm still haunted by those cases."

I didn't know what to say except, "Why don't we call a car service, they have SUV's; we need a giant car and I just realized we need two car seats."

Gypsy was the first one out. She looked like a queen in the wheelchair holding two babies with her subjects around her waiting to tend to her needs. I took Ella from her and struggled to situate her in the car seat. Two teeny babies weighing a total of twelve pounds sure required a ton of paraphernalia. The car seat was a jigsaw puzzle of straps and clasps. Gypsy placed herself between the babies and we waited for Grand; waited and waited.

"Do you think I should go up to see what's keeping them?" I said leaning into the window of the backseat. Camille was helping Grand with her belongings and the discharge paperwork.

"Look." Gypsy pointed over my shoulder. I turned to see Grand and Camille coming through the hospital lobby. Grand was making a fuss over being asked to remain in the wheelchair until she left the hospital. Yikes, it was so unlike her to cause a scene. I wondered if she was suffering from some after effects of her illness. When everyone was finally settled, the driver started the car and as if on cue, Isaiah started to cry. It was a high-pitched scream that accompanied us through the park, down Central Park West and across to Broadway.

Nick, the doorman was beaming like a proud grandpa while he unloaded the trunk. Flowers by the truckload, plants and baby gifts in boxes filled the lobby. I had no idea who all these friends were who had sent so many gifts. I'd never met any of them. We really needed a moving van, I thought when the maintenance crew arrived to help.

We shoved ourselves into the elevator and made our way upstairs. The door was ajar, just like it was on the day I'd arrived here. The two nurses Camille had hired rushed over to greet us.

"Which one of you is the baby nurse?" Gypsy asked, looking the two of them over. The younger one, a gorgeous redhead named Adriana answered in an accent I couldn't decipher.

"Good, here." Gypsy handed the still screaming Isaiah over to her and took the sleeping angel, Ella into her room and closed the door. Grand reached into her purse, withdrew a wad of cash and handed it to the older nurse. She thanked her for service that was not needed. Grand made her way to the kitchen where Katrina was preparing lunch. I collapsed onto the soft leather sofa in that same stressful fashion I did on my first day here. I didn't have much time to figure out how I was going to handle all of this.

"Hey, J, come in here and look at this."

Adriana, whom I learned was from Minsk in Belarus, had finally calmed Isaiah. He and his sister were sleeping in utero style, entangled in each other's space. It took my breath away and I felt a tug I didn't want to be feeling. Not now, maybe not ever.

Days turned into weeks and then months burst by, leaving me with the feeling that barely a moment had passed. The twins were in the ninetieth percentile for weight and height according to their pediatrician. To me, they seemed like they were becoming, turning, slowly evolving into the humans they were supposed to be, rather than developing within some statistical norm; kind of like me. They didn't do a lot of baby gurgling, there was, however, a lot of looking going on. It was as if they were studying their surroundings, soaking it all in. I was in a state of constant amazement. They smiled freely and often, unlike their mother who was anxious to return to her modeling career.

Adriana agreed to stay on as a full-time, live-in nanny/nurse. Grand was happy with her too. She was convinced Adriana found herself in Belarus by way of Ireland with her red hair and blue eyes. Gypsy had immersed herself in an exercise regimen. She imposed strange dietary restrictions on herself that would make a saint surrender to the dark side.

"How about joining me at the gym, they're looking for members?" Gypsy's newly acquired commitment to fitness was becoming an obsession. She tried to recruit everyone who stood still long enough.

"No, Gypsy, I can't. I'm in school full-time, even summers." I was on the fast track, trying to finish college early and get into law school.

PART FIVE

Chapter One

Three years passed by in a flash. I was so entrenched in studying I barely noticed when undergrad came to an end. College life was not much of a departure from high school, in fact, it seemed to be an extension of it. Once again, I found myself to be the outlier in the social order. Under those circumstances, along with the chaos at home, where I oversaw the care and feeding of both young and old, I had no interest in attending graduation. Grand had recovered nicely from her illness and was free from lingering ailments, with the exception of a psychological need to spend every night sleeping in her reclining chair.

"My bed is an heirloom. Your grandfather and I bought it in Europe on our honeymoon. I want you to have it and I don't want you to be afraid to sleep in it because it was my death bed."

"Oh my God, Grand, what a weird thing to say; you need rest. How can you sleep in that chair every night?"

"Never mind, I'm fine." Grand waved me off with one hand.

Home wreaked havoc with my studies so much I considered moving out. I needed to study for the LSAT's. Grand wouldn't listen to my plan to relocate even if it was temporary, instead she moved me into a studio apartment one floor below where I could study in peace and still remain under her roof in a "one foot in, one foot out" way. I took Gracie with me but now she was bungee-corded between my place and home. She'd spend most nights sitting by the door hoping I'd release her from this oppressive small space and take her back to her puppyhood home where she belonged. I felt like a bad parent.

"C'mon Gracie, let's go home for a visit." I took Gracie up the stairwell without a leash. I used my key and opened the door. I heard voices coming from the den on Gypsy's side of the apartment. She had a friend over. I felt my face redden. Gypsy was my only friend, my rock, and I just assumed I was the same for her. I opened the door and stuck my head inside.

"Hey Jenna, this is Jude Mazzei." I stared, stunned. He didn't seem to recognize me. He just said, "Nice to meet you."

All I could think of was how I never even bothered to ask him what his last name was. I couldn't have found this man whom I'd been obsessing over for all these years if I'd wanted to. Now here he was, oh my God, I felt faint. Jude Mazzei had a nice ring to it. Then the toilet in Gypsy's bathroom flushed and out came a gorgeous woman, obviously a model. She sat down close to Jude, very close.

"Jenna, this is Mary. She's Malay, like me. We work together."

"Hello," I said. She merely nodded slightly and I backed up toward the doorway, pointed the index finger on my right hand behind my left shoulder and said, "I'd better get back, lots of work to do."

"K," Gypsy said without looking and returned to the conversation she was having before I'd arrived. I couldn't get back to work, all I could think about was how Jude was sitting there, after all these years, in my grandmother's house and he didn't even recognize me. Had I changed that much? New York City wasn't so big after all. It was just a big small town where everyone knew everyone else or would at some point.

I didn't know what bothered me more: Jude not knowing me, Jude being with another woman, Mary Mazzei having a better ring to it than Jenna Mazzei or the fact Gypsy had other friends. It felt like it was raining rocks all over me. But the fact was Gypsy and I led very different lives. Another fact was Gypsy's modeling career had branched off into commercials and soap operas and she had had several roles on made for TV movies. She was the new face on commercials in everything from shampoo to breakfast cereal. I knew nothing about that world. I was not a part of it. She was rarely home. Adriana was more mother to the twins than nanny. I could see the train wreck ahead, but I survived with less mothering than this and so did Gypsy and Grand too, for that matter. I left all these subjects to stew in my overloaded brain.

Gypsy, on the other hand, had no reservations about meddling into my life. An hour later, she appeared at my door. She didn't mention her friends and neither did I. She fingered Gracie's fur and said, "So, are you ever going out on a date?"

I was tempted to answer, "Are you ever going to stay home with your kids?" But instead, I said, "I don't have the time for dates. I have tests to take, law boards to study for."

"I have the perfect guy for you." Gypsy had a new boyfriend and he apparently had a cute brother.

The boyfriend was president of an entertainment company I'd never heard of. He appeared to be successful, always sending gifts and cars to take Gypsy shopping. Gypsy fantasized about us being sisters-in-law. Not me, I was on a mission to finish what I'd started. I didn't need any more distractions than I'd already had. While this was sort of the truth, there was more to it I didn't want to admit even to myself. I was afraid; parts of me had eroded because of my emotionally stormy past. I still saw Dr. G once a month, but year after year of therapy had not penetrated or healed that part of my damaged psyche. And even if it did, I wondered if I'd forever be dragging this baggage around with me. No matter how busy I was, when there was a lull, it came back in a torrent. Dr. G recommended biofeedback. I was not sure how it worked or if it worked but I was considering it. For now, it was during those *why me* times, when I started to wonder if there were other women out there who had led parallel lives to mine, who had no exit strategy, no rescuing relative waiting in the wings, who had no way out. I wondered if there was some way I could ease my own pain by trying to relieve someone else's. I would have mentioned all this to Grand, but since her *incident* (she refused to call it a stroke,) she had turned into a bit of a curmudgeon. It was a relief sometimes to have my own place to escape to, but I did miss being with the twins.

I thought for sure, Gypsy would have moved out once her career got back on track and took off, but she didn't. Isaiah and Ella gave Grand a new lease on life; it was a relief and a pleasure to have them with us. They called her, *GG—great grand* since Adele was technically their grandmother. Adele preferred to deny all references to her grandmotherly status. She rarely visited but when she did they called her, *Adele,* I was *J,* and Adriana was *A.* It was like alphabet soup.

Chapter Two

Another three years flew by with almost a quicker pace than the last three, and law school was over. For me, it was just a ratcheting up of intensity. There was no time for cliques or girl hierarchal rankings, we were all too busy. As a result, my social skills were still not honed. The extra-curricular offerings in law school were limited to stress relievers like meditation sessions and yoga. I signed up with reservations. Meditation was more effective in helping me through my post-trauma than the biofeedback Dr. G had suggested. Meditation calmed me, was portable and now I could self-soothe. I vowed to continue.

The part-time job in Grandfather's old firm I held during the little down time I had during the summers turned into a full-time position after I passed the bar. That was the extent of the nepotism. My hours were long and the work was tedious, consisting of reading boring legalese. I was not happy at work but at least I was working. Most of my former classmates were working as paralegals or salespeople in department stores.

The long days turned into nights and back again. Gypsy was still obsessing over my nonexistent love life. She couldn't seem to find a man of her own dreams, never mind one for me. I couldn't even conjure up a man of my dreams. I did think about Jude every now and then, but my dreams were clouded and overloaded with work/study ideas and proposals. There was no room for romantic notions. When memories of Jude bubbled up, fatigue diminished the feeling. Now that I was a lawyer, I had access to court records. I was tempted to search for him, to find out what happened, to learn the after effects of the phone call I had made back then. I thought about it, but I didn't want to know any more about it than I wanted to know the current status of Alan J. Rose.

Chapter Three

"Certified letter for Miss O'Connor," the doorman announced through the intercom, "Needs a signature."

"Tell him I'll be right down," I informed Katrina. I'd moved myself back home with Grand, Gypsy and the kids after law school was finished. The twins, now seven, were an amusing distraction from my work life. Gracie was restored and seemed younger than her eight years.

The letter was in an official looking envelope with a return address from the court in California. I was afraid to open it, so I waited until I was safely back upstairs. When Grand heard me scream, she got herself up, uncharacteristically from the recliner and ran to the entryway.

"He's getting out."

"What? Who?"

"Alan, who else? He's only served seven of the thirty-five years he'd been sentenced to and now he's getting out of prison. How could this happen? It says here, he's being compensated for agreeing to aid federal prosecutors in the investigation of some of his former cohorts who'd been trafficking illegals from Mexico and South America. Apparently, Alan's been participating in some undercover sting operation where he solicited the children of illegals by offering the parents asylum in the United States in exchange for the use of their children in illicit activities. He pretended to be working on behalf of his former *perv* gang. In other words, he's a snitch."

"This is terrible, but try not to worry, Jenna, he won't come here."

"I'm being notified, Grand, not asked, not consulted, just notified. I'd have been better off if they never told me this. It says here he'll be a registered sex offender and he's subject to a supervised release but he's going to be free. They are being lenient with him, not only because he cooperated, but because the prison is overcrowded. I can't believe this. Didn't they know it was overcrowded when they sentenced him? It's like he's being rewarded, meanwhile, I'm haunted for the rest of my life, remembering what he did to me."

I'd learned enough about criminal law to know a little about Rule 35 motions and Proffer Agreements. Alan would have had to have provided substantial help to the Feds for them to let him out. But what kind of system did we have if crimes could be negotiated and justice was up for sale? Where was the integrity? I felt the anguish rising up again. How was it a slime, like Alan, got out and battered women who killed their abusers were still incarcerated, sometimes for life?"

"Now, Jenna, he isn't going to bother you. He'd be a fool to do that."

"Listen, Grand, he is a fool, but I can handle him now if I have to, but I don't want to deal with this anymore. I never got any answers. Meghan threw me away like an old rag; she never had to face up to her part in this, not really. She showed up at my high school graduation, did you know that?"

"No, I didn't."

"I was encouraged that day, I expected something, like we'd turned a corner but instead I got the same old Meghan. And on top of everything, she never had the decency to tell me who my real father is."

"Maybe she doesn't know. But maybe it's time to ask."

"I don't want to talk to her."

"Maybe Camille will. But be sure you want to dredge it all up again. Is there some benefit to be gained by knowing the truth? If she'll even tell the truth, how would you know?"

"I don't know. I just feel like my life is so fractured. I need to find a purpose, a reason I was meant to be and a reason all of this happened to me. Does that make any sense, Grand?"

Grand didn't answer, she'd fallen asleep in her recliner. It had become a habit with her. But I knew what she would have said, *you'll find your way, it takes time.*

Chapter Four

The realization that the kind of law I was doing in Grandfather's old firm was not the kind of law that I was meant to be doing, gargled around in my head, first swishing and then finally being spit out. But the recognition of this fact, that had hovered in my subconscious for months, had now been detonated and it rose up to the surface, fueling my suppressed dissatisfaction. I took my disembodied self to my computer where I typed up a lengthy combination thank you/resignation letter to the powers that be in the firm and then went out to the living room to show it to Grand. I didn't give myself time to create any faux scenarios in my head where she would chastise me or where she'd attempt to force me to remain in service to my long dead grandfather's legacy. I woke her up and handed her the letter I'd already placed in an unsealed envelope. Her response was astonishing.

"Good for you," she said before sealing the envelope and handing it back to me.

"What? You aren't mad?"

"No, I'd be mad if you stayed there. I knew you'd never be happy there. You have to find your own niche and it isn't in a big law firm. Give yourself time and you'll figure it out."

The partners in the law firm weren't surprised either when they received my resignation. Despite my being a devoted member of their team, they had sensed my unhappiness. They came one by one with well wishes and offers of anytime advice as I cleared out my desk. I passed through the revolving doors in the lobby and stood in the sunlight on Lexington Avenue and said out loud to no one, "Now what?"

For now, my now what consisted of short city walks with Grand and taking the twins for after school ice cream and the occasional cartoon movie, helping them with their homework, catching up on reading and wondering when my life was ever going to start. I'd been so distracted by the news about Alan, the decision to quit and the angst over being idle for the first time since I got here, I didn't notice until now how frail Grand had become.

Chapter Five

The cab ride to the doctor's office on the East Side of Manhattan was interminable. On the streets where the traffic was light, there was either construction or a garbage truck or a huge potted plant blocking the street. It was an attractive and ecologically appealing addition to the dingy blocks of concrete, but still it was another highly impractical souvenir gifted to the city by the former mayor. It prompted curses and I witnessed at least one near fistfight as the flow of traffic came to a screeching halt after there had been an almost clear shot across town. I placed myself in meditation mode, attempting to prepare myself for the impending worst on my horizon.

People watching was usually enough to spark my creative juices, but this time I was searching around for parolee, Alan. I imagined Alan, after having schmoozed his parole officer, turning him into his best bud, coercing him into joining him on the hunt for Jenna. I knew it was an unlikely scenario given Alan's newly found position as Good Samaritan in service to his country, but still I felt uneasy.

The doctor was a no-nonsense, unfriendly sort who spent all of three minutes with Grand before sending her off to his lab for blood work. I took myself to the waiting room where I perused his year-old magazines. Now I could safely say I was up to date on the latest happenings with the Hollywood set. Gypsy used to be my informer of all things jet set but now she was one of them and she took the entertainment world for granted. I wondered to myself if I'd ever act my age. I felt so old and out of touch. I was not really all that interested in the things typically associated with my age group. Might be because I'd spent my formative years modeling myself after literary characters. I tried to be less formal, less stiff, but still I couldn't seem to pull off the tough New Yorker persona, not yet anyway.

Grand entered the waiting room and checked out at the front desk. The receptionist didn't look up but informed Grand she'd be calling her in a few days to schedule another appointment to go over the test results.

"Will you please call us a cab? My grandmother is weak and I don't want her to be waiting out on the street."

After releasing an annoying sigh, the receptionist grabbed the phone and punched the numbers in hard, as if making a point. I reminded myself to sign up for *Uber.* Grand should have called her driver, but she seemed preoccupied. It didn't cross my mind either, but I was still not used to rich.

Chapter Six

It took three days for the doctor's office to call summoning us to return the following day. This time, Grand arranged for her driver to take us. The buzzer rang at 9 a.m. and the doorman announced the arrival of the car. Gypsy rushed from her room carrying a disposable coffee cup in one hand and her purse in the other.

"You're up early; do you have another shoot today? You were out so late last night, I thought you'd be sleeping in today for sure."

"I'm coming with you."

"Oh, thanks Gypsy."

"You're my family, don't thank me."

The driver followed the same tedious path across town. This time, the waiting room was packed with elderly patients in various stages of decrepit decline. Most were in wheelchairs and were being assisted by women in matching pink pseudo uniforms. We waited for over two hours before Dr. Charisma, my new nick name for him, made himself available to us. We were ushered into the inner sanctum where he sat behind a relic of a desk that was littered with papers. He didn't look up—must be a virus going around—this impoliteness.

He muttered a faux apology for keeping us waiting so long and glanced briefly at Grand before he said, "I want you to see a hematologist/oncologist sometime next week, if possible." He summoned his assistant and together they escorted Grand to x-ray. Gypsy and I were left alone in his office. As soon as the door closed, Gypsy rose, moved to the other side of the desk and sat in the doctor's chair. She flipped through the papers on his desk and opened Grand's file.

"What are you doing?"

"We need to be prepared in case it's bad news. Don't you want to know?" The truth was I didn't, but I didn't tell that to Gypsy.

"Look at this." She pointed to a line on the open page. "R/O Chronic Lymphocytic Leukemia."

"Oh my God, Gypsy! What does R/O mean?" I pulled out my phone and Googled it. There it was—medical lingo for *Rule Out."* I pulled myself together by taking deep breaths.

"Maybe it's wrong, Gypsy; let's go to the waiting room." It couldn't be true, I told myself over and over.

"Don't mention this to Grand," I whispered to Gypsy, who gave me one of her, *give me a break* looks.

When Grand finished and we were settled back in the car, I put on as deceptive a smile as I could under the circumstances and said, "So where do you think the doctor got his training from, some leftover Gestapo medical facility?"

"Oh, I know what you mean, but I was his father's patient; he was a lovely man, but he retired. I should have found someone else but I never got around to it."

I stared out the window; all thoughts of Alan had diminished now, they were replaced by a new terror.

A week later, the hematologist, a super nice, pretty, classy woman in too high heels named Dr. Wendy Whitman, came into her waiting room and escorted us into her office. It was only Grand and me this time. Gypsy had an audition for a television pilot. The doctor was friendly, yet professional in a soothing way as she explained the findings to Grand.

"Here's a requisition for a CT scan; I can schedule it for you. How about tomorrow if there's a time slot open?"

"What's the urgency, Doctor? I'm just a little tired. I'm old, you know, over eighty now."

"Mrs. O'Connor, your blood work shows some abnormalities. Your hemoglobin is quite low and your white count is significantly high. Let's see what the scan shows, if anything, and then we can talk some more, okay? Get some rest."

Four days later, we were back in Dr. Whitman's office.

"Mrs. O'Connor, I would like to take a sample of your bone marrow, stick a needle in your hip and do a biopsy, okay? Your granddaughter can wait here, no need for her to sit in the waiting room, it's a depressing sight in there sometimes."

I was already feeling depression drifting over me like a cloud that had appeared out of nowhere. I knew this wasn't going to turn out well; I could sense it. An hour later, Dr. Whitman came out of the treatment room with Grand in tow. She was holding the doctor's arm like they were old friends. Dr. Whitman was the polar opposite of Gestapo doc. I had moved to the waiting room because I was too nervous sitting alone in the inner office. Dr. Whitman saw me and waved, gesturing for me to follow her and Grand. I walked slowly behind them feeling like I was going to the executioner.

"I'm going to tell you what I suspect but have yet to confirm, okay?" Before she had a chance to finish, Grand piped up with, "Chronic Lymphocytic Leukemia, right?"

"Yes, as a matter of fact," Dr. Whitman seemed flustered like someone just pulled her diagnosing rug out from under her.

"Yes, well I may be old, but I can Google as well as anyone else. Fatigue, weakness, paling complexion, over sixty-five, it all adds up."

"But you know, Mrs. O'Connor, if this turns out to be the case..."

"Yes, I know, I'll most likely die with it than from it. It's not a great life ahead though, you know, being tired all the time; can you give me something?"

"I'm not a fan of Chemo for someone of your age, even though you appear to be otherwise healthy. Let's wait and see what the biopsy shows."

The biopsy came back positive, as expected, and Grand was told to rest and was instructed to avoid crowds where she could potentially contract a life-threatening infection in her weakened state. Avoiding crowds in Manhattan would require her to remain indoors and I was wondering whether it was wise to have her around the twins. They were walking, breathing, petri dishes; most of the time their noses were running simultaneously, oozing yellow gunk. I wondered if I should mention this to Gypsy.

Taking deep breaths had become my normal breathing pattern. It seemed to help me to avoid the panic attack I'd been meaning to have. I took another and told Grand, "I think I'm going to ask Gypsy and the twins to move out, you know, so you can rest and not be exposed to the germs the twins carry home with them." Grand didn't answer, instead she glared at me, shook her head no and I got the message. If she was going to die, she was going to die on her own terms, living the life she'd been living all along. She was not going to adjust according to any illness. Removing the twins would break her heart. Together, they were a bubbling love fest, always giggling little kid belly laughs. Her old lady happiness resonated through tearful laughter when she was presented with the most recent form of seven-year old hilarity. Who was I to mess with that? It was in the hands of the universe now.

Chapter Seven

Every afternoon, once they'd had their snack, Adriana brought the twins in to spend some time with Grand. Grand planned her nap around 1 p.m. so she could be awake and ready when they'd come barging in at 3:30.

"GG, no let me tell her." Ella was the bossy one and slightly taller than Isaiah. She looked like her mother with those copper colored eyes. Isaiah was a mystery, didn't look like James or Gypsy. He was a sweet little boy but always in the shadow of his sister.

"Why don't you both tell her," I suggested trying to give Isaiah a leg up. "Go and practice whatever it is and come back and tell her together when you get it right." Thirty seconds later, they were back.

"GG," they said together.

"Yes, babies."

"We're not babies."

"To me, you are."

"We're trying to tell you something." They both fidgeted impatiently.

"Okay, I'm sorry, tell me."

"What do you call cheese that's not yours?"

"I don't think I know that one, what?"

"Nacho cheese," they shouted and all three of them broke into fits of hysteria. I rolled my eyes and left them to it.

In reality, there was nothing to distract me from worrying day and night. I was up and wide-awake every morning at 3:37. I wandered around in the darkness of my room until I found my way to the window seat, then I sat and looked out the window at the street lamps and started the nighttime ritual of over thinking. I wondered if Grand was scared, if she was panicked like me or at peace with herself. I wondered if she'd lived the life she'd wanted or if she had regrets.

"Stop hovering," she told me out of the blue one morning when I asked her if she wanted her breakfast on a tray.

"Go and find yourself something to do; do some pro-bono work until you figure yourself out. I have plenty of things here to keep me occupied. You don't need to be watching me every minute for signs of rapid deterioration."

"Okay, Grand, I'll look into some pro-bono work."

"I already have. Camille gave me the name of a child advocacy group looking for a lawyer to do pro-bono work a few days a week. Here's the information; it's perfect for you, for right now. And maybe you'll meet some nice young man."

Now it was my turn to glare at her. I'd never told her about Jude but now it seemed there wasn't really anything to tell, still I thought about him a lot, all these years later. I wondered if it was true how you'll never forget your first love. If that's even what it was.

Chapter Eight

No interview was required for pro-bono work. Camille did all the preliminary introductions, all I had to do was show up. It was 8 a.m. on Monday morning when I arrived at a dreary looking building on the lower East Side. A woman in a dated brown flowered skirt, which dangled halfway between her calf and her ankles, greeted me with a half-hearted good morning and showed me to a cubicle. The desk had two short piles of papers in files on either side of its chair.

"Oh, not too bad a load," I said while fanning one of the piles. I turned to look at the woman who introduced herself as Ida and saw her point to the opposite end of the desk. There on the floor were four stacks of files, each standing at least two feet high. "Oh," was all I could think to say. I might be here for decades reviewing these cases.

"Check these out and see if anything can be done for these kids. Legally, you know," Ida told me. She walked away with a swish of her skirt.

It was 4 p.m. before I realized I hadn't eaten all day. The caseload was not only daunting, it was heart-wrenching. I found myself so entrenched in the narratives that read like novellas on the subject of abuse and neglect that I'd barely made a dent in the first pile. There were stories, one after the other of kids who were imprisoned for fighting back, for stabbing or assaulting their abuser after being exploited for years. New York State, in its sophistication and infinite charity, had deemed children to be adults at the age of twelve; it used to be seven. Funny, I always thought the brain wasn't fully developed until the age of twenty-five. I was on the cusp now, at twenty-seven.

There were no community-based alternatives in place for these kids. Maybe this was my new mission, what I'd been wallowing around waiting to find. Then there was the foster care debacle. A few of these kids were in loving homes with intact families who were anxious to adopt them but their druggy incarcerated mothers wouldn't release them. I couldn't help but compare them to Meghan who eagerly seemed to throw me away. Then there were the kids who moved year after year from one foster home to another. They had no stability at all; they changed schools every year until they aged out at eighteen. I vowed to give each of these files my best effort, for as long as it took.

"I just got a call, this kid needs an advocate, any interest?" Ida asked handing me another folder.

"I'll bring it home and have a look at it." I was barely out of childhood myself. How I was equipped to be anyone's advocate totally escaped me. I excused myself for the night; I was concerned about Grand.

I need not have worried about Grand. I heard multiple voices coming from the apartment as I approached the door. There she was in the recliner, just where I had left her, only now I could barely see her. She was surrounded by at least ten of her "dearest friends." I'd been here a long time now and I'd never met or heard about any of these people. A surge of guilt emerged bringing nausea along with it. All these years it had been all about me. I never even thought to ask Grand what she did to occupy herself for the seventeen-plus years before I landed in her lap. I just assumed she taught cooking classes and that was it. But here was the proof in the flesh of her former life without Jenna. There sitting next to Grand was a refined gentleman, whom if this were a 19th century novel scenario instead of a 21st century living room, he would have been called, "Debonair." Wow! He was tall and had a full head of thick white hair and dark blue eyes, and he was wearing a navy-blue suit. He had Grand's hand in his; she pulled it away when she noticed me staring. It was funny, she was acting like a nervous teenager. Turned out, they were all staying for dinner.

Katrina announced dinner was served and the eleven of them piled into the dining room. Grand's table sat twelve. Luckily, Gypsy was out with the twins; it was pizza night.

I wondered how all this activity came about without me knowing a single thing about it. Grand sat herself at one end of the table and motioned for me to sit at the opposite end. Mr. Aidan Duffy escorted me to my seat, pulled my chair and pushed me back in, giving me a jolt. He was a charmer; I liked him, in spite of myself.

"Jenna, this is Mrs. Anderson, she's a widow like me. Her husband was a real estate tycoon here in New York. He started his business in the 1920s. He was a lot older than we were. We all looked up to him. He gave wise investment advice. Isn't that right, Irene?"

Mrs. Anderson's excessive jewelry dangled loosely against Grand's fine china. She nodded in response to Grand's question while asking me to, "Please pass the Beef Wellington, dear." It was clear she wanted the subject changed.

Grand continued the introductions and gave a brief bio of each guest after Mrs. Anderson dismissed her. To my amazement, I learned Grand was president of several charities; she also served on the boards of hospitals and corporations. I felt like I was an observer on the outskirts of an alternate universe. I also got a lesson in decorum while observing their impeccable table manners and politeness which didn't let up. They seemed to be showering the room with an overabundance of nice bordering on *this can't be for real.*

Every woman here was a widow, I learned as Grand regaled me with information about deceased husbands and their former professions and net worth over sorbet and cookies. I wondered what these women did for all those years while their husbands were out amassing fortunes.

"We're a W.O.W.," Grand said laughing, "A world of widows." And one widower, I assumed although Grand seemed to have skipped over Mr. Duffy's history. I excused myself and went to the kitchen to help Katrina with the clean-up. It was late.

"Where did all these friends come from all of a sudden?"

"Oh, Miss Jenna, she's the best friend to all these people. Your grandmother, you don't know, she was there for them whenever they needed her and now she needs them."

"But I've never seen any of them before."

"She's devoted to you now; it's not like Mrs. to make you feel less important by having all these people around."

"It would've been okay."

"Oh, Miss Jenna, Mrs. was so happy when you came here. It was like the answer to a prayer. She didn't need anything else or anyone else. But these people, these friends, they love her too. She's given so much to so many people; never did she ask for anything. Now they think she needs them so they are here."

"What about Mr. Duffy?"

"Oh, year after year, Mr. Duffy asked Mrs. to marry him, but she wouldn't."

"Why not, do you know, Katrina?"

"Sometimes, when I'm here late, I ask her and she said to me, *one man in a lifetime, is one man too many.* She's a funny lady, your grandmother."

"I guess." But this was all news to me.

The dishes were cleared and tucked away into the two dishwashers for the night, unlike the widows and Mr. Duffy who were in the living room enjoying glasses of Port. Grand was on the sofa now, looking pale and worn out.

"Nice to have met all of you, finally. I have some work to do so I'll say goodnight now," I told them, hoping they'd all get the hint and go home.

"Goodnight, dear," they all seemed to say with one voice.

I returned to the kitchen to forage for something to eat. I stopped eating meat a year ago and didn't eat the Beef Wellington at dinner. There was leftover pizza in the fridge that Gypsy must have put there when she got home. She had to have snuck in with the twins unnoticed to avoid the W.O.W.'s. Sometimes, I swear, she had a sixth sense or maybe she knew stuff I didn't. After all, she had been here far longer than I had. I tiptoed into the twin's room where they were sleeping soundly and angelically in their bunk beds. In another year or so, they'd be asking for separate rooms. But for now, they were still babies and were content to be together. Gypsy's light was still on; I knocked lightly on the door.

"Who is it?"

"Seriously, Gyps."

"Hey, Jenna, what's up?"

"I don't know, just feeling weird. Grand has all these friends, this whole life I knew nothing about and now she may be dying."

"So, you've met the widows; and Aidan, isn't he hot for an old dude?"

"Ew! Really Gypsy! He's got to be eighty-five years old."

"So, Kate is what--eighty? You think he's too old for her? What's wrong with you?"

"I don't know. She never told me about any of these people."

"She probably didn't want you to think you were intruding on her life here. You'd been through enough."

"Was I? Am I, intruding on her life? Do you think?"

"Are you crazy? Your grandmother adores you. She came to life when you got here. I used to come up for dinner sometimes when Adele was away and the nanny du jour was preoccupied. Kate is one of the most selfless, kindest ladies I know. The widows are just acquaintances of hers. They're nice enough but they're no substitute for you. Or even me, I think, or even the twins. You know, even if you never came here, I think Kate would have helped me anyway and taken us all in. It's amazing to think how we all ended up together. All those years ago when we met in the elevator, who would have thought we'd end up being a family?"

"Thanks, Gypsy."

"For what?"

"For being my family." Gypsy stood up, stretched her arms up over her head and let out a yawn. I got the hint.

"Well, I guess I'll let you get some sleep."

"Yeah, I have a shoot in the morning and I don't want to look pasty for the camera."

It was after midnight when Mr. Duffy left with the nine widows. They weren't exactly quiet on their way out. They laughed and yelled out goodbye. It seemed they were collectively deaf. When I finally heard the door close, I got up and went to check on Grand. She was already asleep in the recliner. I reminded myself to talk to her about this insane sleeping arrangement. I was going to promise her I wouldn't be *creeped out* sleeping in her heirloom bed. It wasn't exactly going to be the truth, but it wasn't entirely a lie. It didn't matter to me where Grand died, I'd be honored to have memories of her around me. But the bed was a monstrosity; it belonged in a Baroque exhibit at the Met, not in someone's apartment bedroom. I couldn't imagine her liking it, never mind buying it and shipping it half way around the world. There had to be a story attached to it. It was a story I'd never get to hear.

Chapter Nine

Katrina was the one who found Grand. She'd decided to serve coffee in the den when Grand didn't come out to the kitchen for breakfast. It was the morning after the dinner party, rendering it the last supper in my mind. I couldn't shake the feeling that all the commotion had been too much for Grand in her fragile state. She seemed to have been snuffed out like a candle. She got her wish: she died peacefully in her reclining chair.

Katrina called Camille first and she was the one who told me. The sun was barely up when I heard a knock on my door. When I saw Camille, I knew.

Grand had put "her affairs in order," Camille told me. "She did it long before she was given her diagnosis. *At my age, I could pop off at any minute,* she told me when we were writing up her new will." The doctor had been called and the funeral home representative was here. I felt numb and sick to my stomach. It was another nightmare. Gypsy and the twins were sequestered in their side of the apartment. Every once in a while, I could hear one of them sobbing.

Grand wanted her funeral to be held at the childhood church she had attended when she was living with her Aunt Eileen. It was the one in the story of Jimmy and his dying days. It would take a few days for us to get things in order. I had a little time to prepare a eulogy of sorts.

There were so many people attending Grandmother's funeral, the police had to close the street from Broadway to Amsterdam Avenue and loud speakers had to be staged on the church steps. I looked around at all the people heading inside and thought how I didn't really know much about my grandmother at all.

I thought I saw Alan in the crowd, but a second look proved that notion to be wrong. Camille had called Meghan; her number was disconnected and no new number was given. I wondered how some people could spend their lives perpetuating grudges and hate, even into death.

In a few minutes, I'd be the one giving the eulogy. While gathering my thoughts a few nights ago, I called upon the *Mistress of Death*, Emily Dickinson for inspiration. Grand had specifically requested I be the one to say a few words. Emily Dickinson knew about dying and how to do the mourning of it. She had feared death her whole life but death often paid her a visit. Her bedroom window in her childhood home in Amherst, Massachusetts, had overlooked a cemetery. Death carriages would parade by carrying the old as well as the young, dead before their time from some affliction for which a cure had not yet been discovered. Emily was obsessed with death; she, like me, was more at ease with grief. She wrote:

I can wake Grief
Whole pools of it-
I'm used to that-
But the least push of Joy
Breaks up my feet-
And I tip-drunken-
Power is only Pain
Stranded, thro
Discipline-

It was joy, I decided, that was unreal to me, fleeting like being drunk; joy couldn't last. But no one would understand my way of thinking. They'd say *you're grieving, in mourning,* and my all-time favorite, *it takes time.* I was a motherless, now grandmother-less child-woman, nearsighted by grief; I couldn't look ahead. How was I going to do this?

Reading an Emily Dickinson poem about her dealings with death would—in essence—make Grand's funeral about me. Instead, I chose two of her poems about the obscure dead.

One dealt with a woman dying at play; this was in keeping with Grand dying just after her dinner party. The other described death as an adventurous journey to a strange land. Camille read one poem and Gypsy, wearing a black hat and her signature sunglasses, read the other. I went up to the altar as soon as Gypsy finished.

"For those of you who may not know me, I'm Jenna O'Connor, Katherine's granddaughter. I don't know most of you and as I look around at all of you and those of you who are standing outside, I realize you all probably knew my grandmother longer and perhaps better than I did. Perhaps, you have more of a right to your tears than I do. As Camille read in the Dickinson poem, I imagine Grand is now experiencing: *The divine intoxication-Of the first league out from the land.* What I did know of my grandmother was she wasn't one for staying still. It was Pasternak who wrote: *To live life is not to cross a field.* There was kind of a breathlessness to Grand's life. No obstacle was impenetrable. The fractured domesticity of her childhood years did not define her. She had a profound acceptance of whatever life handed her. She was always quietly busy with a new project, a new student cook, a new charity, a new real estate venture, a new something else. While her doctor had said, she wouldn't die of her illness, but rather with it, I knew it would cause her death. It would cause weakness and she would be unable to do all the things she loved and she simply could not live without doing all the things that were on her horizon. When her life disassembled itself, and seeped out of her capable controlling hands, she left us for a new one."

I stopped briefly to take a sip of water and looking out over the audience, quickly realized it was not a good idea. The audience looked bored; they probably had no clue what I was talking about. But this wasn't for them, it was a tribute to Grand. I took a deep breath, put my head down, looked at my notes and continued speaking, "My grandmother, whom I didn't know as well as most of you did, in a very short time, made me a better person. She made me whole. Grand held an air of indifference to the past. She taught me to shed my troubles, to put them behind me, not to wear them through life like out of date garments. Yet, now as I step firmly into adulthood and reluctantly into her shoes, I would say, rest well, Grand, but I know she can't do that. She's more likely to already be organizing heaven's kitchen. Thank you." I stepped down off the altar.

The usher came to the lectern after me and said, "Thank you for coming and please join us for a reception at the Metropolitan Club, located on the corner of East 60th and Fifth Avenue.

Transportation will be provided."

I wondered if Grand knew her funeral would be a sellout. She had requested buses be provided; she'd requested the ballroom of the club be used for her post funeral reception. The ballroom held over 400 people. Even though the club had waved its dress code, people showed up impeccably dressed out of respect for the woman who had given most of them a leg-up in life as one man had explained to me. Many people stopped to speak to me; I didn't see most of them. I was looking through an opaque lens.

As I was about to walk through the carved oak double doors at the back of the church into the waiting limousine, I heard a man's voice, "Hello Jenna." I lifted my bowed head, I was stunned to see Jude staring back at me.

I was chilled to the bone. I didn't know what to say, other than, "What are you doing here? I thought you didn't recognize me? I thought…" Camille came up behind me just then and took my arm. "We have to go now, Jenna."

"Wait, this is Jude, Camille, he's a friend of mine from California. I need him to come with me. Is that okay?"

"Sure, Jenna, you don't need my permission, you can do whatever you want."

Camille nodded hello to Jude and we walked together down the church steps.

When Jude took my hand in his, time was suddenly erased. We were as we once were, all those years ago when we met on the lake's shoreline. It was as if nothing had happened. It wasn't the time for a reunion, or for catching up on years gone by, but Jude insisted on giving me a synopsis of his life and what happened to him since I had last seen him. I heard his voice, but most of his words just floated through the air without reaching my ears.

Gypsy placed a glass of wine in my hand. "What's Jude doing here?" Jude had left to get a plate of food.

"He's from California, I knew him there."

"How come you never told me about him?"

"I never told anyone about him, there was nothing to tell." I lied.

"Must be something to tell, he's here."

"Yeah, but he's with your friend, Mary"

"Not anymore, they broke up," Gypsy said, raising her eyebrows before going in search of Adriana and the twins. The wine calmed me somewhat and I was ready to hear what Jude had to say and to find out what he was doing here.

"I had the impression you didn't recognize me that night."

"You look the same. I never stopped thinking about you. I came here to pay my respects, to see you and to ask you something."

"What's that, Jude?"

I knew what he was going to ask me. I was terrified but then I thought things must have turned out okay considering he was here and looking incredible in his expensive three-piece suit. I knew I wouldn't be able to handle an altercation on this day of all days. I glanced around for Camille or Gypsy or even Mr. Duffy but they were all entrenched in conversation and didn't make eye contact.

"Was it you who called the cops on us that night?" I swallowed hard, trying to keep the tears welling up in my eyes from falling, but Jude put his arms around me and pulled me into them.

"It's okay if you did, Jenna, you saved my life."

I thought I was vulnerable back then, when I first met Jude, but I felt more helpless now. With Grand gone, I had nowhere to lean. It was like I'd lost the ground beneath me.

Leaning on an old boyfriend, who was briefly a part of my life, at this time, would be just as risky as it would have been to run off with him when I was seventeen. I needed time, again; I needed time to heal and to grieve.

The priest came in to say a prayer signifying the end of the reception. I'd hoped it would go on forever, so I wouldn't have to go home and face the loss of Grand head on. Jude handed me his business card, kissed me on the cheek, said goodbye and left, but not before glancing back with a sweet smile on his face.

Chapter Ten

I sipped tea; I couldn't eat. Grand had lit a spark in me, and now it was extinguished. Despite the sweltering August heat, I was cold. I dressed in long pants and a sweater and whenever I could, I held onto the twins. Grief had blindsided me. It was so acute. Dr. G said it was different than mourning. Grief hit hard while mourning was a subtle constant. I forgot the ADLs-activities of daily living, like eating, washing my hair and breathing. It felt like I'd been holding my breath since Grand took her last.

It would be my job to deal with the aftermath, to go through Grand's things, file her away like old news and then do what? The old fear of the unknown was back, hovering like thick air refusing to dissipate. With it came pangs of regret and then the 'what if's' followed behind. What if I had tried to wake her when I went to check on her that night? Maybe I should have called EMS, then maybe she would have survived. Didn't I arrive here so Grand wouldn't have to die alone? But she did die alone and in the damn reclining chair. I wore my grief like a sickness.

Nights were the worst, alone in my room. I flipped unasked questions through my mind like a Rolodex. How long had she been lying there dead in that chair? When I went to her, after finding out she was dead, she looked like she was just sleeping peacefully. I later learned from Camille, Katrina had graciously closed Grand's eyes. It had been a generous act of kindness toward us all. In the dawn's light, I lay wondering about the religious concept of the afterlife. If it was true, Grand was somewhere. If she was somewhere, maybe I could conjure her up.

I walked around in this dazed state for three weeks until Camille took hold of me by the shoulders and stated rather emphatically, "Life does go on, Jenna. I've given you time, now we need to read the will and make some plans and adjustments." I had no idea what she was talking about. I drowned myself in books by Edgar Cayce. His books contained hopeful premonitions about life after death, reincarnation and soul evolution.

"It's something to hold onto," I told Camille when she found me reading a book he co-wrote with his son. It was called, "No Death."

"I have something you can hold onto."

"What's that?"

"It's the pro-bono job I stuck my neck out to get for you and what's this?" she asked holding up the child advocacy file I'd forgotten all about. Along with my personal neglect, I'd left a needy kid beached on the crowded shores of social work hell.

"I feel inert, can't someone else do it? I'm facing a *bizarre confusion of directional signals at the crossroads of passing time with all the no-longers of one world corresponding to the not-yets of the other.*"

"Well put, Jenna."

"Not me, Nabokov."

Camille frowned. "Okay, Miss Lit, who do you suggest I get to take over your pro-bono job?"

"I don't know, just not me right now."

It was only 8 p.m. but I took an Ambien and plopped myself down on my bed. "I need to sleep, Camille, please can we talk about this tomorrow?"

Camille closed the door behind her with the same gentle touch that reminded me of Grand. Would everything remind me of her, in some way from now on? I fell asleep with those thoughts filed among all the other unanswered questions still in my head.

Six hours later, I woke up with the remnants of the drug-induced dream swimming around. Dreams fascinated me, if only I could linger in that world. Last night's Ambien dream starred Grand and Katrina cooking in the kitchen, like in the good old days, only this time they were not teaching student cooks, they were force-feeding Meghan Kelly, the former anchorwoman from Fox News. She was pleading for mercy. Then Nicole Elliot from horror high school burst in asking where I was? All of them responded at the same time, even Meghan Kelly joined in saying, *she's off wallowing.* Then I woke up. It had to be a message from Grand. She hated wallowing as much as I hated the word. I pictured her at the foot of the throne of the supreme being demanding a shot at sending a message to the loved one she'd left behind. It was the first laugh I'd had since Grand died. Wallowing was what I was doing. It was early, but I got up and grabbed the file of the kid who needed an advocate. It read:

Luca Manchera, age eleven is the son of former drug dealer and Trinitario gang member, turned informant Vincent Manchera, who along with his wife, Maria were shot gangland style in their own bed. Luca was visiting a friend that night and was spared. He is now in the custody of his maternal grandfather, attorney Mr. Dennis A. Martin. Luca is being adequately provided for in accordance with specifications stated in the will of Mr. Manchera. A guardian ad Litem needs to be appointed to oversee the distribution of the trust and to represent the interests of the child.

Luca's file sat on my desk while I tended to Grand's estate. The bulk of it was left to me with a substantial trust for the twins and a nice inheritance for Gypsy and Katrina. Meghan was completely excluded. Camille was executor of the estate; it was sizeable with investments, property holdings, stock options as well as cash and jewelry. It was daunting.

I hadn't entered Grand's room since the night she died. I supposed her clothes remained in the closet or folded in the drawers and her toothbrush sat in the holder on the side of her sink, waiting for her to start her day, while her ashes resided temporarily in an urn on the fireplace next to the pictures of me, Gypsy and the twins. Grand was staunchly organized. Her affairs were in order, as they say, and her bills were all paid. Yet, here were her ashes waiting for her inept granddaughter to figure out where to put them.

Chapter Eleven

Before Katrina left for her Thanksgiving break, she placed Grand's ashes on a shelf in the kitchen. She told me, "This was Mrs. O'Connor's favorite room in the apartment," but I knew Katrina was secretly hoping Grand would offer some inspiration as I attempted to prepare my first Thanksgiving dinner. She didn't. If she was present it was merely as an observer. I could almost hear her gasp as I turned away from the stove for a second; it was long enough for the butter to melt too fast. It smoldered and half of it crept along the edge of the pan obliterating the mushrooms, which I had added too early. The recipe said, *add a splash of brandy.* When I did, it flamed up, smoldering again as it rose to the ceiling in a smoky mass. The mushrooms lay ruined in the designer pan; kind of like me, I thought.

I stuck a fork in the bit of mushroom I thought I could salvage and brought it tentatively to my lips. I took a small bite, grinding it between my teeth into miniscule test model bits. Mushrooms, I learned, as a rule, took on the flavor of their host dish. This batch had all the taste suffocated out. It tasted like ash, only Gypsy would say, *ass.* I dumped some of it in the trash. I put my head in the refrigerator willing a new box of mushrooms to appear when the door opened and Gypsy came in with the twins lagging behind.

"They're delivering the turkey at 2:30," she announced as she placed the grocery bag on the counter. "It'll be cooked and ready to eat. They gave me stuffing in a separate container, it needs to be reheated. Would one of you brain trusts close the door? Please!" The twins had a habit of leaving the apartment door open.

"Don't call them names, Gypsy." I immediately regretted interfering, she gave me one of her, *I know what I'm doing* expressions.

A long time ago, I thought Gypsy knew everything. And I knew nothing back then. I thought I needed her to guide me, but maybe I just needed her to ground me. I was afraid all the time now. She was busy with her career. Grand was gone and I was alone.

At almost twenty-eight years old, I should at least be capable of preparing part of Thanksgiving dinner, but I was fumbling to provide a grandmother-like splendor to a sorely lacking celebration. It was a struggle to hold back tears, to try to keep up the appearance of family for the sake of the twins, to demonstrate life went on, and to keep my guilt at bay. Grand died in August, and I had yet to find an honorable place to put her remains. I'd yet to go into her room to sort through her belongings. I didn't know what I was afraid of; I didn't know what I thought I'd find. I guess it was closure which scared me the most. Once her things were gone, it would be the end of the story. I'd wait until after Christmas. Maybe something would come along to sideswipe that plan, I hoped.

Chapter Twelve

James' Christmas presence at the door was the last thing we expected on Christmas night. The doorman, who was most likely distracted by residents laden down with shopping bags, had left his post and James just wandered in and up the waiting elevator to our apartment. It took him nearly ten years and Grand's death to suddenly have pangs of fatherly regret. Gypsy stood in the doorway, she wouldn't let him in. She was giving him poisonous looks. I studied his demeanor from the sidelines. He appeared somewhat disheveled, yet he still held his head with the same arrogant, superior stance. He oozed self-absorption and I didn't blame Gypsy one bit, for saying, *So, were you notified of my sudden inheritance? Is that why you crawled out from the cracks? Where's Madeline, by the way?* Gypsy had become the rich girl James had always assumed she was, but now that she'd been worn down by life, she'd wised up and was more self-reliant, less needy.

"Just want to see my kids."

"Get out! They don't even know you exist."

"What did you tell them?"

"That they are special and were designed by heavenly beings and sent to me. You had nothing to do with it, now get out." The door closed and like the ending of a bad movie, James faded to black.

"He is their father, Gypsy. They're going to ask questions, one of these days, you know."

"Yeah, so, any rodent can be a father. You should know that more than anybody. They don't need him, they have us."

Gypsy was right; James was an opportunist and no more capable of change than Alan or Meghan or Adele. We were better off without any of them. I needed to shake off my idealistic view of matters and be more of a realist. The twins didn't deserve a father like James.

Chapter Thirteen

I was trembling when I opened the door to Grand's bedroom. It was an irrational reaction, I knew but since her death in August, the room had remained an ever-present foreboding reminder. Her belongings had been left untouched like relics in a shrine, while life went on outside the closed door.

The heirloom bed, made up with white linens tautly held in place with surgical precision, rose up in glacial splendor like an old chariot and seemed to be watching me from its post on the far side of the room. I wondered if Katrina had been coming in here all along, dusting and tidying up. Katrina stayed on with us after Grand died, even though she had enough inheritance to support herself for the rest of her life and beyond.

"Work is what I do," she told me when I asked her if she was going to retire. I knew if I'd asked her to, she would have cleaned out Grand's room for me. But it was something I had to take on myself. The absence of Grand was so profoundly present in this room, it was torture. I felt uneasy fingering Grand's clothes, like I had no right. When I opened the top drawer of the large chest, I found an envelope addressed to me on the neatly arranged cotton nightgowns.

Now Jenna, don't get maudlin in here doing this. It has to be done. Don't give the good stuff to just anyone. Katrina might like to have one of my coats. Keep some trinkets for yourself, Gypsy and the twins. Make peace with the heirloom bed; it will be priceless someday. And please forgive my intrusion into your new beginnings.

All my love from above (hopefully,) Grand

On it went, Grand controlling the distribution of her no longer needed belongings from beyond the grave. I couldn't help but laugh, but what did she mean by, *my intrusion into your new beginnings?* I guess I'd find out.

Her clothes were immaculately clean and her suits, while dated, looked as if they were purchased yesterday. On the floor in one of her closets, I found a case of the long defunct *Sweetheart Soap,* the soap Grand had said, *you couldn't kill.* I reached in to take out a bar to try for myself, but I felt like a thief and hesitated. Its scent was filling the room.

All of this is yours, now Jenna; you will figure it all out in time. I sat sheepishly on the heirloom bed and read the P.S. part of the letter. The mattress was surprisingly soft, I lay down in reconciliation. "You win," I told it before I fell asleep.

The next morning, I invited Gypsy and Katrina to look through Grand's possessions. Gypsy had not one flutter of curiosity, "Nope," she said, "I don't need to wear her to remember her. Give it to charity, that's what she would've done."

Everything except for two winter coats, the furniture and jewelry was given to the *Sloan Kettering Consignment Shop* to sell; the proceeds would all go to the pediatric ward.

I moved into Grand's room. I still had to tackle her desk. The papers, while organized alphabetically, still overwhelmed me. I began to organize them according to what I could handle and what should be sent over to Camille.

In the P file, I uncovered the mystery of Grand's cryptic note regarding *my new beginnings.* There in plain sight was a receipt for the services of a private investigator. Grand had hired a private investigator to find out who my father was and it was the same investigating firm who had trailed my mother when she went MIA from her parents before she was pregnant with me. They had found not only her whereabouts, but also whom she kept company with at that time. It seemed that a few months ago, they had resurrected the case and retraced their long-ago steps. Somehow, DNA was obtained from me and my biological father and here it was in black and white—the name—Dennis A. Martin Esq. In the bottom of the file, on a piece of scrap paper, was the name and phone number of Ida Barkin, MSW.

Chapter Fourteen

Even though I had more answers now than I did before, I was still wondering why? Why all the secrecy? Why did Grand maneuver us all around like pawns on a chessboard? Why not just tell me, ask me to give a DNA sample? And why didn't she explain herself in the letter? Maybe she thought she'd have more time. I couldn't be angry at her, whatever her reasons were, I knew she had loved me. She knew she was going to die; she knew I needed answers and she had had the power to provide them. I wondered if she had somehow found out about Jude too. That seemed too far-fetched even for Grand. Now, I had to figure out what to do with this new information. Knowing who my father was hadn't sunk in yet. Another weird feeling bubbled up, a kind of fear of the unknown, fear of more changes, the fear of growing up, and fear of more loss. If I stuck to the ordinariness which had settled in since Grand died, nothing would change.

I decided business as usual was best. I'd yet to meet Luca Manchera, my nephew and his grandfather, my father. I wondered if Dennis Martin knew the truth. I kept busy with Luca's case as if nothing out of the ordinary were happening. I'd been called on to oversee the distribution of his financial wellbeing. Luca's father had set up a trust; no one questioned where the money had come from. I approved a withdrawal for a tuition payment for a private school in lower Manhattan and another one for uniforms and incidentals. If anyone official did some digging and found out I was a relative, this would be called a conflict of interest. I considered consulting Camille but decided against it.

"Luca Manchera seems to be in good hands," I told Camille, who had stopped by to check on things. "I've never met the kid or the guardian, but he seems to have the best interest of his grandson at heart, seeing to his education and stuff. He's the grandfather, right?"

"Yes, Dennis is a good guy."

"What do you know about him?" I asked, trying to fish to see if Camille had any inkling of the truth. I doubted she did, even with the lawyer/client privilege rule, I knew Grand wouldn't have risked telling anyone what she was doing. She'd probably threatened the investigator or had something on him. I bet no one knew, not even Dennis Martin.

"Oh, Dennis lost his only daughter, he'd lost contact with her years ago after she'd married Luca's father. Dennis didn't approve. He'd raised Maria after his wife died. He's had a lot of loss. He never met Luca until after his parents were killed. But Dennis jumped right in and rescued the kid. It's sad but both of them are adjusting. The kid knows who you are though, he saw your picture in the paper, has a bit of a crush, thinks you're a celebrity."

"The celebrity would be Gypsy."

"Okay, Jenna, how about we talk about finances now?"

"Camille, c'mon, you know I hate that stuff, can't you just handle things?"

"Jenna, you're not a kid anymore, you need to deal with this, invest some of the life insurance money, buy some real estate, things like that. You're like an anti-consumer. Look at you in that old stuff you wear, year after year. Get yourself something new, for God's sake. Go out on a date; get out of this rut."

Chapter Fifteen

Grand's friend, Mr. Duffy made it his irritating business to check on *his girl,* as he put it. He did so just about every evening around 8 p.m. He could be counted on like the nightly news. He used to be a resident of the building and was still considered a regular; the doorman let him in without question.

"Here to pay my respects, it's how it was done in my day, dear." I doubted that but said nothing. I found the whole situation suspect, especially after his grandson started joining him on the nightly intrusion.

"Gypsy, don't you find it strange such a handsome man like Mr. Duffy has a progeny as foul looking as his grandson, Barrett?"

"Shit happens," was all she said.

Barrett was an actuary with the hair to match. His black hair was severely parted and plastered to his head with thick gel. If the literary character, Uriah Heep from David Copperfield could have had a look, Barret would be it. He didn't say much, he let his grandfather do the talking. Mr. Duffy prodded him with hints of how nice it would be to *have a girl like me.* This infuriated me and propelled me right back to my commodity days with Alan. Gypsy was unfazed.

"Give him a try."

"Are you serious, why?"

"It's good practice."

"For what, prison?"

"No, for when the real deal comes along or for when that cute guy, Jude comes back to get you."

Every other evening, for weeks on end, Mr. Duffy showed up with Barrett. They only stayed a few minutes to do their routine check. It wore me down; I agreed to a sympathy date with Barrett on a Tuesday night after work at a restaurant on Central Park South.

"Thursday night is date night so Tuesday is perfect," Gypsy notified me.

"Is that important?"

"Yeah, no one will see you."

"But, I don't know anyone."

"Yeah, but someday you might and you don't want them to remember you with him."

"Why am I even doing this?"

"Just go, it won't kill you."

Barrett's underwhelming self was sitting at a long booth facing out. The restaurant was crowded with mostly business people and tourists. I took the chair opposite him. He made no attempt to stand when I came close. He must be adopted, I thought.

"So, what does an actuary actually do?" I asked, trying to jumpstart a conversation.

What a mistake. His life story rolled off his tongue like a world without end. He talked about himself over appetizers, his former self and the exceptional math skills he had as a child, during dinner and his future self who would surely someday be an analytical consultant in risk management for the U.S. Government, during coffee. When the check finally arrived, he took an interminable amount of time scrutinizing it until I grabbed it from him and handed the waiter my credit card. I signed the check while Barrett stared at me like a deer in the path of a four-wheeler. I slid my chair back, got up and headed toward the door.

So, this was dating, I thought to myself as I walked up Broadway toward home.

Gypsy was standing in the doorway when I came in. She had a mud mask on her face and a thing on her head she called a *doo rag.*

"When's the attack," I asked.

"Very funny, how was it?"

"Like kneeling on rice," I said while picking up Gracie's leash and attaching it to her collar.

"She's already been out; the twins took her."

"Well, she's going out again; I need air; I need to reassess my life; I need to clear my head to try to figure out why I felt desperate enough to put myself in the path of that troll, Barrett Duffy."

"Sorry Jenna, I shouldn't have encouraged you to go out with him. I didn't think you'd take it so seriously. I really think there's something you need to understand."

"What's that?"

"It's just you and I are goddesses and it takes a long time to find a god."

"That's it? That's your philosophizing advice? C'mon Gracie."

"Excuse me," I said to the doorman who was reading the New York Post. He looked up at me over his reading glasses and put the paper aside.

"Yes, I want you to make a note for yourself and the staff—please tell Mr. Duffy no one is home when he comes by next time and every other time after that, I mean it!" I raised my voice and put my clenched fist on his perch for effect.

"Yes, of course, Miss O'Connor." The doorman tripped off of the chair, knocking the paper off the perch and ran to open the door for Gracie and me.

Broadway was crowded with after work shoppers and men in suits holding briefcases, no doubt heading home after having had drinks with colleagues. There was not a god among them. I fingered Jude's business card; it was still in the pocket of my suit jacket. *Not yet,* I said to no one in particular.

PART SIX

Chapter One

It was the broken gate attached to the wrought iron fence which attracted me to the six-story brownstone for sale in upper Manhattan. It reminded me of the story Grand had told me when I'd first arrived about the *opening in the fence* feeling she'd had when she barged into Aunt Eileen's life. The stone structure looked decent from the outside. I took out my cell phone to call the number on the sign posted on the front lawn. The grass was brown and the shrubs looked unkempt. The whole place had the appearance of an abandoned puppy, charming but in need of recovery.

"This is Jenna O'Connor, I was wondering if I could arrange for you to meet me at the property you have listed, say tomorrow around 2 p.m." I adjusted my tone and gave it the authoritative flare Gypsy had advised me to adopt. It seemed to be working.

Gypsy still amazed me with her ability to manipulate whomever or whatever came onto her radar. I guess it was a learning process. I headed towards the subway, glancing back over my shoulder at what may turn out to be my life plan.

The real estate agent called back to confirm and gave me the scoop on the property. He called it, *an estate sale.* The recently deceased owner was nearly one hundred when she died. She'd been the last of her family. No heirs would be slithering out of the woodwork to stake a claim. The proceeds of the sale would go to charity.

Despite being cradled in the heirloom bed, I didn't get much sleep. I needed to plan carefully and to get professional advice before I set out on an adventure of this magnitude. The property was assessed at several tens of millions of dollars. Grand had been a master investor; she'd taken whatever allowance Grandfather had given her, and she'd turned it into an empire. I didn't want to be the one to bring it all crashing down. I imagined the headlines: *Granddaughter heiress of Katherine O'Connor's estate loses the entire inheritance in one foolhardy investment.*

Chapter Two

The broker was a nerdy guy carrying a clipboard. He seemed way too nervous to be in real estate or any other sales business. He opened the faded mahogany front door and allowed me access while he waited outside, which I thought was odd. The entry-way was surprisingly wide for an old house; it led to what I supposed they used to call a parlor. It was where gentleman callers would be kept waiting. The floors were dark and splintered and creaked whenever I took a step. The kitchen was non-existent. The previous owner must have existed on take-out; reminded me of Meghan. The bathrooms were equally disastrous. When I turned on the tap, a burst of air escaped before brown water started to flow. I stuck my head out the front door and surprised even myself by saying, "I'll take it."

I'd need to do some preliminary road paving before asking Camille for her advice. Grand had requested I consult with Camille before making any major decisions or purchases, for the short run, anyway. I didn't mind, Grand had known what she was doing. Whatever instructions she'd left for me, I'd follow without question.

Cameron Nelson, the contractor I hired, was a friend of a friend of Gypsy's. He called me, "Mam," which I didn't like. I thought you had to be at least forty to be considered a "mam."

"Mam, this building has good bones; what's needed here is a cosmetic renovation, you know, updating. I can recommend some architects who can sketch out some plans. Then I can take it from there. By the way, if you widen all the hallways and the doorways, the building department will call this a handicapped facility and the permits will be expedited. It's just a suggestion."

"It's a good one, thank you."

"No, thank you, Mam."

"Listen to me, Cam, please call me anything but Mam, if you want this job. Jen or Jenna or J or Miss O'Connor, anything else, okay?"

"Yes, Mam," he answered. I just stared at him.

"Sorry, Ma…Miss O'Connor."

Maybe it was my new wardrobe infusing me with snootiness. Of course, Gypsy outfitted me from head to toe. I looked unreal even to myself, kind of like Audrey Hepburn in *Breakfast at Tiffany's. Holly Golightly* was not a character I could ever be. I never go lightly; I had angst about everything. Even though this new look was awkward at first, it was growing on me and I could sense the power of money following my every step.

"You need attitude; you need an air of sophistication; you need to talk with an authoritative voice in order to get what you want," Gypsy informed me for a second time, as she tweaked my look for the day. "Here wear this, it's a power scarf."

"A what?"

"Just wear it, Camille's tough. You have to have self-assurance if you want to get her swayed over to your way of thinking." I tilted my head to the side and raised my neck up to tighten the skin and pursed my lips in kind of a scowl.

"Yikes, what you need is practice."

"I don't have time to practice; I have an appointment with Camille in an hour."

Chapter Three

"Why so formal, Jenna? You didn't need an appointment, I thought we were friends; it's nothing serious I hope?"

Camille questioned me with concern on her face. I swallowed hard and inhaled deeply before saying, not in the authoritative voice Gypsy made me rehearse, but in a contrite and mousy sounding voice, "No nothing serious, well I'm thinking of buying some real estate and I'd like your thoughts on it. Uh, I guess I've already agreed to buy it and I just wanted to let you know."

I opened my eyes wide in nervous expectation. I'd never bought anything more expensive than a winter coat. This was huge.

Camille listened while I presented not only the history of the building with the *good bones*, but also the plans for the renovations the contractor had suggested as well as the plan for the potential charitable business I hoped to establish after all the work had been completed.

"I see you've done some homework on this; it seems well thought out and the business plan is well written. If you had needed a loan on this, I don't think even the most stringent of banks would have denied this venture. I say go for it. I'm here if you need any help. Congratulations!"

"Thanks, Camille, it's a relief to hear you support me on this. By the way, I need all the help I can get. I don't have a clue what I'm doing. All I have is an idea."

"Yes, but it's a good one, it's worthwhile, sorely needed and provided you aren't too stuck up now in your fancy clothes to ask for help, you'll succeed. I'm glad you've found a niche for yourself. I knew you'd never be happy in the firm. I admire you for trying it. Good luck, just kidding about the clothes. You need to look the part. This look gives you the air of authority you're going to need."

I adjusted my suit jacket, tucked in my half hanging out blouse, fixed the power scarf and thought how Gypsy was still my go-to person for all things relating to how to be.

Once outside, I felt my step lighten; I walked excitedly up Broadway. I now supposed I could be *Holly Golightly if* I tried hard enough to put the past behind me.

Chapter Four

Fat chance of that happening, my past was sitting in the kitchen sipping tea when I got home.

"What could I do? I had to let her in; she just came up and appeared at the door, just like that scumbag James did. We really have to petition to fire that doorman."

"Oh my God, Gypsy, what do you think she wants? I'm going to change; go see if you can find anything out."

"Okay, but can I make a suggestion first?"

"What?"

"Keep your suit and power scarf on, she probably wants money. It's the greatest lure of all time- gets the vermin to come out of their hovels."

I rolled my eyes but I kept my suit on. Not only did I do that, I removed my sunglasses from the top of my head and returned them to the bridge of my nose. I slid them slightly down, exposing my eyes, glared over the rim and said, "Hello Meghan, what brings you here? Are you back for your Amex card? You never did ask for it back."

"I didn't, huh, I must've thought I lost it." There she was, manipulating the truth to suit her purposes. She had to have paid the bill for my escape.

"Yeah, whatever, why are you here?"

"I'm here on business and I thought I'd come by to see you."

"I haven't seen or heard from you since court and you didn't come by to say goodbye or pay respects to your own mother." If she'd shown up to help Grand out, if she had made any attempt to reconcile while Grand was dying, if only she'd been there to support me, I would have cut her some slack.

"That was a complicated relationship."

"Really, what do you call ours?" I didn't let her answer. "What did you do, leave another kid home alone; are you working on screwing up another human being?"

"No, I lost the baby; it was stillborn," she was whispering.

I said nothing. I really wanted to say what I felt in my heart but something held me back. I wanted to say the baby probably had the good sense to choke itself with its own umbilical cord, rather than be saddled with a mother like her.

"Oh, c'mon Jenna, look how well you're doing, let it go. We just got off on the wrong foot."

"Is that what you call it? When did we get off on the wrong foot? Was it in the Delivery Room when I was born? When? I'm your daughter; who's my father, by the way?" I put the question out there just to see if she'd tell me. "Is it Alan?"

"Alan, seriously, it's anybody but. We weren't even married. We started out as friends. He helped me out when you were a baby so I could work."

"Yeah, some help." It was obvious she wasn't going to tell me.

"It was a tough time for me; I was young and vulnerable, trying to get back at my parents, not really a grown up."

"You still aren't. You threw me away to that wolf, left me alone with him, let him use me that way."

"And I paid for all that."

"You think so, Meghan? What do you want? I have no money to give you if it's what you're here for. That would go against everything Grand wanted. I think you should get up on your wrong feet and leave. I'm done."

"So, you won't ever forgive me… ever?"

"Is that what you're here, forgiveness? No, I'm not ready to forgive you, I'll probably never be ready for that."

Meghan got up, put her cup in the sink and walked to the door. Her hand was on the doorknob when she turned around to face me. "I'll be here for six weeks working on a project; here's my card, call me if you reconsider; we only have each other now."

I wondered what happened to Mr. Stanton but I didn't care enough to ask. I was so angry, I couldn't imagine ever feeling any different. I was running out of steam. Gypsy seemed to sense it and I saw her near the doorway. She stepped out of the shadows and put herself between Megan and me.

"How nice to see you again, Meghan. Thanks for stopping by. Just don't ever do it again."

Meghan tried to ignore the comment and stormed out, while Gypsy slammed the door behind her.

I didn't know whether to laugh or cry, but when Gypsy cracked up laughing, I did the same, "Get up on your wrong feet and leave" brilliant, Jenna, I'm going to use that line."

Chapter Five

It took nine months to renovate the brownstone. It was a painless rebirth. The work was largely on the interior so winter did not hamper the progress. The façade was left as is, leaving an air of old-world charm and ambience. The gate was still being temperamental, sometimes closing with ease and sometimes unhinging all together. The gate company, who had first installed it in 1899, went out of business in the 1960s. I didn't want a new one; this one added to the charm of the place. It was reluctantly inviting with its new coat of varnish. The lawn was newly seeded and perking up. Flowering shrubs and border plants completed the look. Temporary signage announced what was coming. To me, it was perfect.

"So, Grand, I know it took me a long time to figure things out. Sorry for the wait, but I think this is the place. It will put you in the middle of things, just where you always wanted to be."

I opened Grand's urn and as I was about to scatter her ashes, I heard, "Who you talking to?" I turned my head and saw a young boy sitting on the side of the only tree that was original to the property. I had a pretty good idea who he was, but I didn't let on.

"My grandmother, I'm talking to her. What's your name?"

"I don't see her."

"I'm talking to her spirit. Are you Luca?"

"Yeah, that's me."

"What are you doing here?"

"I follow you, sometimes, not all the time. I wanted to meet you, you kind of look like my mom did."

"Really, I do?" I felt a surge of excitement, a thrill; Luca had no way of knowing his mother was my sister. I was pretty sure I was the only one who knew. He had no way of knowing the gift he'd just given me.

"Luca, I need to scatter my grandmother's ashes now, and then we can have a chat, okay?"

I opened the urn fully and scattered the ashes around the lawn and into the flowerbeds, "Rest in peace, now Grand. Inspire me, okay? Stop maneuvering."

A light wind picked up, but the ashes remained where they'd fallen. I was at peace too. This part of the city was quieter than down south near home.

Luca interrupted my thoughts. "You know what I think?

"What's that?"

"I think that sign is sexist." He was pointing to the temporary sign on the lawn which said, *The Katherine O'Connor Center for Women and Girls.*

"You think so, why?"

"This place is going to be for women with problems, right?"

"Well, yeah that's right."

"So, what's a woman supposed to do if she has a kid who's a boy?"

"You're very smart, you know that, Luca? I think it's true what you're saying. I'll be changing the sign for sure. Maybe now we should call Mr. Martin. He must be worrying about you."

We headed toward the door when we heard a man's voice call out, "Wait, I'm here." It was coming from the direction of the street. A man with dark, curly hair wearing a rumpled suit was struggling to get the gate to stand upright. He pushed it back onto the hinges and miraculously it stayed put.

"Hi, I'm Dennis Martin; you must be Jenna O'Connor."

He gestured for me to shake his outstretched hand. His dark eyes radiated a gentleness despite the messy suit. I felt an overwhelming sense of relief, an instant connection, like I'd found my way. It was a bizarre gratitude of sorts for being related to this man, even though I just met him. It was all probably Grand up there messing with me. I glanced up for a moment, as if to say, "Stop."

"Nice to finally meet you." He nodded then turned to Luca. "Listen, Buddy, you can't keep running off without telling me. I've looked everywhere for you. I told you we'd arrange to meet Miss O'Connor. She's a busy lady, you shouldn't be bothering her."

Luca didn't look the least bit sorry. He didn't even answer, instead he went over to the tree to climb it. Mr. Martin left him to it while he looked at me with an odd expression.

"Everything all right, Mr. Martin?"

"Yes, sorry, it's just that, well, I know O'Connor is a common name but I used to know a Meghan O'Connor. It was years ago, when I was living in California. Any relation?"

I averted my eyes and turned my head toward the brownstone; the stone façade was glittering in the sun. The echo of Grand's voice resounded quietly in my ears, *safe haven,* she seemed to be saying. I gave Mr. Martin an effortless half smile and turned toward the tree where Luca sat on a heavy branch.

"Yes, O'Connor's a common name." I changed the subject quickly, just like I'd learned from the master.

"Hey, Luca, I heard they delivered snacks and ice cream today, want to check it out?"

"Sure," he yelled jumping off the tree and landing hard. I winced, but he quickly stood and came running toward me. He took my hand without embarrassment. He held it hard, like he too had found something special he wanted to hold onto. As we walked up the steps to the brownstone, I reached over and with my free hand, I pulled the sign out from the grass and threw it face down on the lawn. Mr. Martin rushed ahead to hold the door for us. He placed his back against the open door, but before he let me pass, he turned to face me. "I don't mean to pry, but are you related to Meghan O'Connor? Is she your mother? You don't look like her, but you do sound like her."

It wouldn't take much digging if Mr. Martin wanted to know the truth about me, but for once, I was going to slow things down. If I blurted out the whole truth now, Mr. Martin would think I was a crazy person. I was going to spend as much time with both Luca and my father as I could, before telling them the truth. It would take some getting used to, like everything else in my life had. But when the time felt right, I'd tell them. "It'll be soon, Grand, I promise." I muttered under my breath.

My father seemed to be a persistent man; he wouldn't let go. He had this need to know about Meghan. Maybe he loved her, and maybe it wasn't the one night stand I'd imagined. But since he didn't have the nasty habit of changing the subject Grand and I had mastered, he kept pressing. This time when he asked me again about Meghan O'Connor, I stared firmly into his eyes that looked a lot like mine and I told him straight—it was my grandmother Kate who raised me up.

THE END

ABOUT THE AUTHOR

Joni Marie Iraci is a retired Registered Nurse who raised three children before returning to college in her late fifties to pursue a life-long dream of becoming a writer. She earned a bachelor's degree in liberal studies with a concentration in writing and literature from Sarah Lawrence College before earning an MFA in creative writing from Columbia University at the age of 65. Her short stories can be found in the online literary journals: ReviewAmericana.com and BeneaththeRainbow.com. She is currently working on a collection of short stories about writers and a novel called *The Vatican Daughter*. She was delighted to discuss her incarnation as a writer and the joys and angst of attending college in her later years in a speech at the Rotary Club in Rye, New York. She lives in New York with her husband, two catered-to dogs, a diva cat and four lovable stray cats who wandered into her life. "Reinventing Jenna Rose" is her first novel. Her current website is JoniMarieIraci.com.

Made in the USA
Middletown, DE
11 May 2019